MALICE in UNDERLAND

JENNI JENNINGS

Illustrated by HANNAH PECK

Published in the UK by Scholastic Children's Books, 2020
Euston House, 24 Eversholt Street, London, NW1 1DB, UK
A division of Scholastic Limited.

London – New York – Toronto – Sydney – Auckland
Mexico City – New Delhi – Hong Kong

SCHOLASTIC and associated logos are trademarks and/or
registered trademarks of Scholastic Inc.

Text © Jenni Jennings, 2020
Illustrations © Hannah Peck, 2020

The right of Jenni Jennings and Hannah Peck to be identified as the author and illustrator of this
work has been asserted by them under the Copyright, Designs and Patents Act 1988.

ISBN 978 0702 30440 8

A CIP catalogue record for this book is available from the British Library.

Printed by CPI Group (UK) Ltd, Croydon, CR0 4YY
Papers used by Scholastic Children's Books are made
from wood grown in sustainable forests.

1 3 5 7 9 10 8 6 4 2

www.scholastic.co.uk

For Lily, Hugo, Amelia, Oliver
and Jacob, with love.

MISCHIEF WAS
THEIR BUSINESS

The Malign family were early risers. It was half past seven on Sunday morning and most of them had been up making mischief for hours.

Now, the Malign family weren't just making mischief for fun. Mischief was their business and the business of mischief was a very serious matter. As representatives of Underland – land of sorcery, spooks and skulduggery – it was their responsibility to maintain respectable levels of gunge and ghastly

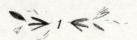

amongst the Topsiders.

Topside was the ordinary world, where alive people lived out their lives, blithely unaware of the mischief being concocted in the shadowy world below. The Underlanders called people who lived in the ordinary world *Topsiders*. The Topsiders didn't call the people who lived in Underland anything because they didn't know they were there!

Ma and Pa Malign had been to the boot fair with Malice's little sister, Antipathy-Rose. Pa had crept between the cars, letting all the air out of the traders' tyres. Ma had sneaked about the stalls, stealing all the best trinkets. Antipathy-Rose had sat cooing in her pushchair, biting passers-by who stopped to admire her. It was a perfect morning of mischief.

Malice Malign on the other hand, had stayed at home. She'd promised to catch up on her mischief-making later. So, while her family were out robbing and biting, Malice was secretly reading.

I say *secretly reading* because Malice's parents didn't approve of reading one bit, unless it was to read maps pertaining to buried treasure of course. Malice had also had a good long soak in the bathtub. She would keep that a secret too. Ma was a great believer in the virtues of minimal bathing; she liked to keep behind her ears good and dirty, so the earwigs had somewhere to nest.

The rest of the family returned, laden with loot after a hard morning's mischief. A large bag of swag spilled out over the kitchen table. Ma stood at the sink buffing a monolithic moonstone ring. Her tights fell in baggy wrinkles at her ankles so that her stick legs looked like turkey necks. Every few seconds, she would jump and shiver, and let out a *squeak!* as droplets of icy water from above dripped down her back.

"That's enough, Grandad!" Ma yelped, banging her hand down on the draining board. "I know it's you!"

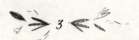

3

Malice mooched into the kitchen.

"Oh, Malice, thank wickedness!" cried Ma. "Tell Grandad to pack it in, will you? He's made himself invisible again!"

Malice looked up. In the far corner of the kitchen ceiling, squished up above the sink and giggling, was her favourite ghost in the universe: Grandad. Grandad was dipping his hand in and out of a glass of iced water and flicking drops down the back of Ma's neck. He had a mischievous grin on his crinkly face.

"Hello, Grandad," said Malice. Grandad hadn't made himself invisible to her.

"Hello, Ducky," said Grandad, looking down from the ceiling. "Fancy a game of poker later?"

"Absolutely." Malice grinned. "You won't beat me this time!"

Grandad grinned back and flicked his wrist again to let loose a shower of icy water down Ma's collar. Ma screeched.

"Ma wants you to pack it in," said Malice apologetically. She knew Grandad was just having a bit of fun.

"I'm not deaf!" said Grandad. "I'm ignoring her on purpose."

"All the same," said Malice. "It's probably best to give it a rest."

Grandad sighed.

"All right, Duck." Duck or Ducky was Grandad's pet name for Malice. "But only 'cos it's you what's asking. This house used to be fun!" he added sulkily and disappeared up through the ceiling.

"I'll see you later for poker," floated Grandad's disembodied voice.

Ghosts have the power to make themselves seen or unseen. Grandad had chosen to remain unseen by Ma and Pa, ever since they'd fed Malice's history project to Antipathy-Rose – who had enjoyed it immensely. Grandad felt sure Malice would have got an "A" for it, had her parents not been so spiteful.

Malice loved her grandad; he understood her. She only wished she had more time to spend with him, so that he wasn't on his own so much.

Grandad had been a ghost since before Malice was born. He could have gone to live in Underland, but he'd had the feeling that young Malice would need an ally growing up in Malignant House. And

he'd been right. Apart from being alive, Malice had absolutely nothing in common with the rest of her family.

Ma dabbed her neck with a tea towel and picked another stolen ring from the swag bag. It was gold with a big creamy pearl in the middle. Ma rubbed the pearl against her yellow teeth and cackled.

"Real!" she announced with glee. "That'll fetch a pretty penny when we flog it."

Malice turned to leave the kitchen, but Ma called her back.

"Malice, you're on mischief duty today," she said.

"But, Ma, I've got homework to do," Malice complained.

"Homework!" shrieked Ma. "Homework! Don't let Pa hear you talking like that. We've been over this. Nuffink nice never came to no one what did homework!"

Antipathy-Rose began to scream in her highchair. Ma went on. "You need to pull your weight, young lady! There's mischief to be made and I've got four new ghosts in the oubliette waiting to be processed. We can't do it all! Pa is exhausted and I'm just about at the end of my rag."

The oubliette was a windowless, doorless dungeon where Ma and Pa held their newly recruited haunting ghosts before releasing them on to the unsuspecting public.

Malice's sister continued to scream. Her highchair began to levitate and spin.

"Antipathy-Rose Malign, I swear that racket is melting my brain box!" yelled Ma, holding her head.

Antipathy-Rose's round face was screwed up around a dummy she had clamped between her sharp little teeth. She clutched a doll between angry fists. Her curly black hair was sweaty from her tantrum.

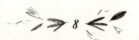

Antipathy-Rose had the kind of face that made adults go all gooey and start talking in silly high-pitched voices. Her chubby cheeks were rosebud pink and peachy soft, her eyes were round as marbles, framed with long black lashes, and her lips were a perfect heart shape. It wasn't until the gooey adults stuck their big cooing faces up close to hers that Antipathy-Rose smiled to reveal two rows of pointed teeth – sharp enough to make a shark jealous – and snapped at their sticky-out noses.

Malice walked over to the howling child. She yanked the dummy out of Antipathy-Rose's mouth and threw it out of the kitchen window. Then she wrenched the doll from her sister's chubby hands, ripped off its head and one of its legs, and dropped its dismembered body on to the highchair table.

Antipathy-Rose stopped screaming instantly. The highchair bumped back down to earth. A creepy smile spread across her tear-stained face and she cooed happily as she played with her doll's remains.

"You've got such a way with her," said Ma. "I don't know how you do it."

Malice shrugged.

"Now off with you!" Ma shooed Malice out of the kitchen. "Get out there and cause some mischief!"

THE SUN NEVER SHONE ON MALIGNANT HOUSE

Malice walked out into the sunshine. Felicity Square – the very nice neighbourhood in which Malice's family home, Malignant House, was considered a bruise upon the landscape – was calm and quiet.

Malignant House was impossibly gangly with more gables and turrets than is seemly in polite society. The tips of the turrets were shrouded in a black cloud that permanently loomed over the Malign residence. Knotted brambles and snaking ivy

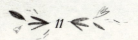

 climbed the crumbling walls and wrapped themselves around broken balconies and decrepit verandas. The sun never shone on Malignant house and the many grimy windows reflected only shadows and the occasional pale face pressed against the glass.

Meanwhile, the residents of the tall, white, pristine townhouses, who reluctantly shared Felicity Square with the Maligns, were still tucked up in their beds, enjoying a pleasant Sunday lie-in. Malice sighed and began to make mischief. She picked up a stick and half-heartedly dragged it along the railings surrounding the Felicity Square gardens. A row of headless sunflower stalks lined the flowerbeds,

victims of her parents' twilight mischief mission. Malice shook her head. She did not enjoy mischief, at least not the kind that Ma and Pa encouraged.

Malice enjoyed merry mischief, like sneaking biscuits from the pantry, or throwing waterbombs out of windows, or seeing how many ornaments she and Grandad could balance on Pa's protruding stomach while he snoozed on the sofa.

The sound of Malice's stick on the railings rang out into the peaceful morning, clanging like a one-noted xylophone. It disturbed a flock of birds, which rose squawking from the old oak tree. Dogs began to bark. Malice kept dragging the stick.

A Bentley with a personalized number plate was parked outside Number 6. Malice kicked one of the wheels hard with her boots. The car alarm squealed.

Sleepy faces emerged from behind curtains of brocade and velvet, their morning breath clouding the cold glass of the windows. Malice shrugged her

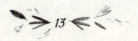

shoulders at them apologetically.

"Sorry!" she called, embarrassed.

The bed-headed residents scowled at her and wrenched their curtains shut. To them she would always be *one of those dastardly mischief-makers!*

If it was up to Malice, she wouldn't make mischief at all, but she didn't want to let her parents down. Ma had been nearly heartbroken when she'd caught Malice recycling plastic bottles. Malice felt permanently stuck somewhere between wearing the goody-two-shoes or sitting on the naughty step.

The sun glinted off Malice's wild raven hair and her shiny black biker boots. The emerald green stripe in her tights perfectly matched the colour of her bright, intelligent eyes and complemented the stripy top she wore beneath her black pinafore dress. Her cheeks weren't rosy like her sister's, nor were her teeth pointed, but they shared the same turned-up nose, like a ski jump for fleas.

In the far corner of the square a mountain of russet and gold leaves quivered in the gentle breeze. The Felicity Square Residents Association had spent a fun Saturday afternoon sweeping, scooping and heaping the fallen leaves into one big pile for collection by the council.

The Malign family had been pointedly absent.

"Disgusting!" Pa had said, watching them from the window.

"Community spirit?" said Ma. "Makes me sick to my stomach!"

Malice had watched the proceedings from the attic window. She had so wanted to be a part of it, especially when the residents' association held a BBQ for all the helpers and they listened to music and ate burnt sausages beneath the orange October sky.

Malice's reverie was broken when Seth cycled into the square on his bike. Seth was a paperboy and Felicity Square was on his round. More importantly,

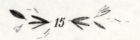

he was Malice's best and only friend.

Maligns didn't have friends. It was forbidden. Malice's parents didn't want her mixing with *none of those tender-brained Topsiders*. They didn't want her *mischief mojo messed with by them matey-friendship weirdos*. But Malice couldn't seem to help but be friends with Seth; they'd been *weirdos* together since the first day of school.

"Hallo, Malice!" he called. "How's it going?" Seth was practising wheelies; he was very good at wheelies. He picked up speed as he rode around the square, pulling his front wheel up between pumps on the pedals.

In reply, Malice grinned mischievously. She carefully aimed the stick she'd been dragging along the railings at Seth's front wheel and threw it hard. The stick stuck in the spokes. Seth and his bike catapulted through the air and landed in the leaf mountain, which swallowed boy and bike whole with a swooshing sigh.

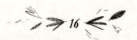

The leaves, so carefully swept and scooped, erupted into the air like tangerine lava and fluttered down like amber ash all over the square. Ma and Pa would be very pleased with the mess of leaves covering the ground once more. Malice thought, *If I must make mischief I might as well make it fun!*

Seth and his bike were completely invisible inside the leafy volcano.

"Don't you like him?" asked a voice, curiously.

It was Vexatious Malign, Vex for short: Malice's uncle. He was leaning up against an old oak tree.

"He's my best friend," said Malice.

"That wasn't a very nice thing to do to a best friend," said Uncle Vex.

Malice narrowed her eyes at her uncle. "Wait," she said.

The heap juddered and shuddered, and suddenly Seth exploded out from its centre, grinning widely. He shook himself free of the crispy leaves and hauled his bike out.

"Thanks, Malice!" Seth beamed. "That was brilliant! Can we do it again?"

"Maybe later," said Malice.

She cast a sideways smile at Uncle Vex, who had made himself invisible; his quivering, translucent

form melted into the rough bark of the oak tree. Each Malign was born with a magical gift. Uncle Vex's happened to be invisibility. He'd also soaked up a lot of Underland magic during his years living among the ghosts.

Magic is absorbed in the same way as a yawn can be infectious or someone's bad mood can be contagious; you just sort of pick it up as you go, like chewing gum on the bottom of your shoe. Seth followed Malice's eyes to where Uncle Vex stood, but saw nothing except the ancient tree. He shrugged.

"Righty-ho," said Seth. "I've got to finish my paper round anyway. Ooh, that reminds me…"

He pulled an old newspaper from his satchel. The date at the top read 1982.

"For Grandad," said Seth. "He said he wanted to catch up on old news. I found this in the library archives. There's some great hairstyles in there!"

Seth's hair was the colour of golden straw and so messy – even when he hadn't just been catapulted into a leaf pile – that it looked as though someone had rested a bird's nest on his head and forgotten to remove it.

Malice rolled her eyes and took the newspaper. Sometimes she thought Seth was weirder than she was.

"Thanks, Seth," she said. "He'll enjoy that, he's read everything in the attic at least twice."

Most people would be horrified to find out that Malice had a ghost for a grandad; Seth was delighted. There wasn't much that flustered Seth. When Malice had first told Seth that she lived in a haunted mansion and could do magic, she had been worried that he might not want to be friends with her any more. But Seth had just shrugged his shoulders and said, "Cool!" and offered her a chewy fruit sweet. To Seth, ordinary was overrated.

"Did you hear about the graveyard?" he asked.

"What graveyard?" replied Malice.

Seth looked pleased to have news that Malice hadn't heard yet. A smile stretched across his freckly moon-face.

"They've discovered an ancient graveyard!" said Seth. "Can you believe it? They were digging the foundations for the new shopping centre across town and they unearthed a cemetery! I was cycling past and stopped to have a look. I heard one of the archaeologists say it was Roman. And you know what that means, don't you?"

"I do?" asked Malice.

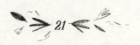

"Skeletons!" Seth said with glee.

"Obviously," responded Malice.

"Have you ever seen a real skeleton?" asked Seth.

"One or two," Malice said.

Malice's house had a skeleton in almost every cupboard.

"Can you show me one?" Seth asked.

"Sure," said Malice.

"Cool," said Seth. "Well, I'd better push off. I've got to help my dads cook dinner when I've finished my paper round."

"Are you still up for moth practice tomorrow after school?" Malice asked.

"Sure am!" said Seth.

Seth jumped on his bike – a red chopper, his pride and joy – and began to cycle away.

"Catch you later, Malice!" he shouted.

"Not if I catch you first!" Malice called after him.

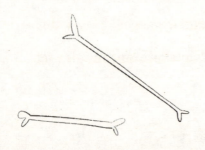

NOT A USUAL MALIGN

Seth's laughter echoed around Felicity Square as he rode out of sight. Uncle Vex peeled himself off of the oak tree. He was a tall man, with a frame so spindly that his head looked unfeasibly large; physically, he resembled a rather well-dressed wooden spoon. Unlike most Maligns, Uncle Vex was meticulously clean and well presented; he always wore a perfectly pressed three-piece suit, his hair was gelled into a stiff quiff that stood thirty centimetres off his head, and he smelled of lavender soap.

"Maligns don't *usually* have friends," said Uncle Vex, brushing bits of moss from his suit jacket. Uncle Vex was Pa's younger brother, though there wasn't much of a family resemblance.

"I'm not a *usual* Malign," said Malice.

Uncle Vex smiled. Uncle Vex didn't enjoy making malicious mischief either. Vexatious Malign was a private investigator in Underland. He solved mysteries and righted wrongs. This made him extremely unpopular with the rest of the Malign family.

"Are you teaching Seth to *moth whisper*?" asked Uncle Vex.

Malice could talk to creatures that came out at night. That was her magical gift. It took practice, of course, any skill worth having does, but Malice was happy to put in the time. She was often to be found in the evenings having a chat with a bat or a mooch with the moths.

"What if I am?" asked Malice.

"No reason," said Uncle Vex. "And Grandad lets Seth see him?"

"Yes," said Malice. "What of it?"

It was rare that a ghost gave an ordinary person permission to see them. It was even more rare for an ordinary person to be able to learn Underland magic. But then, Seth was not quite ordinary. Grandad had been happy to give Seth permission to see him, even if it was only waving at the windows or chatting through the rusting filigree ironwork of the Malign property gates, while Ma and Pa slept off their mischief-making. Seth had never been into Malignant House.

"Isn't it a little unusual for a Topsider to be mixing with Maligns?"

"Not *all* the Maligns," said Malice. "Just me and Grandad."

Uncle Vex nodded. He was more open-minded

than most Maligns. Uncle Vex had parted company with the family when his lack of shifty acumen became intolerable for everyone involved. He undermined their mischief at every turn and the family were in real danger of getting a good reputation because of it; he had to go! But Malice knew Pa kept a photograph of his estranged younger brother, folded up in the secret compartment of his wallet.

Uncle Vex lived in Underland with the ghosts and ghouls and all things, well, dead. He'd tried living in Topside but found he preferred the company of ghosts; dead folk were less judgemental than the living and they were far more appreciative of his fashion choices.

"You're probably wondering why I'm here," said Uncle Vex. "I'll get straight to the point."

"I wish you would," said Malice.

"There's trouble in Underland," Uncle Vex said matter-of-factly. "I need your help."

"My help?" questioned Malice. "Why?"

"Because you're smart and because I need someone who's good with ghosts."

Malice frowned, unconvinced.

"And," continued Uncle Vex, "because I think the Malign Haunting Agency might be involved."

Malice felt her stomach flip over. Her parents ran the Malign Haunting Agency. She wished they didn't. In return for buried treasure, Ma and Pa transported the dastardliest ghosts out of Underland and released them into nice Topside houses, with respectable Topsider families, and let them haunt the bejeezus out of them. Their business wasn't strictly in keeping with the Topside Public Relations Handbook, but the Underland council were prepared to overlook it to be rid of some of the more troublesome ghosts. The four ghosts presently waiting in the oubliette at Malignant House were so despicable that the Mayor of Underland himself had

sent a telegram of thanks to Ma and Pa for taking them off his hands.

"Why do you think the Haunting Agency is involved?" asked Malice.

"Ghosts are being disappeared," said Uncle Vex. "They're being sucked out of Topside without a trace. All of them grandad ghosts, interestingly."

"Ma and Pa's business is putting ghosts *into* Topside, not sucking them *out* of it!" said Malice.

"Indeed," said Uncle Vex. "But I've been hired by the Cosy Grandad Agency because their grandad ghosts are being disappeared." He looked uncomfortable. "Given the rivalry between their two businesses, it does suggest foul play!"

The Cosy Grandad Agency was in direct competition with the Malign Haunting Agency. One wanted to soothe Topsiders with sweet dreams whispered by cosy grandads, while the other wanted to scare the pants off them.

Malice bit her lip. Surely her parents wouldn't stoop so low? They were more crooked than a crook selling stolen watches on the corner of Pilfering Street, but they wouldn't be involved in grandad-napping, would they?

"I could really use your help, Malice," said Uncle Vex. "You're the smartest Topside Malign I know."

Malice considered the trouble she would be in if she was caught helping Uncle Vex. "A hideous henchman of helpfulness" was how Pa referred to him. Helping anyone at all was bad enough but helping Uncle Vex! Well, that was worse than getting an "A" in a school report.

"I'm sorry," said Malice. "I can't help you. I'd like to. Honestly, I would. But I can't."

Uncle Vex shook his head in disappointment.

"Sooner or later you're going to have to start being true to yourself, Malice," he said. "You're not cut out for a life of mischief-making."

Malice shrugged.

"Ma says you're a bad influence. She says, *Maligns don't help nobody and nobody helps us.*"

"Not even when helping is the right thing to do?" asked Uncle Vex.

"Especially not then!" replied Malice. "I'm sorry. Pa says, *We look after our own kingdom, let somebody else look after the others.*"

"Sometimes helping other people is the best way to help yourself," Uncle Vex said persuasively.

"And sometimes it's the best way to get yourself into a heap of trouble," Malice countered.

Uncle Vex sighed and handed Malice a small black card. On one side were the words:

And on the other:

FOR HELP WHISPER HERE

"Keep it," he said. "In case you change your mind. I'll be in Underland continuing my investigations."

And with that he stepped back behind the oak tree and faded into nothingness.

Malice sighed. The trouble was that she wasn't a full-blown Topsider like Seth but nor was she a full-blown Underlander, what with her being alive and all. Technically the Malign family – including Uncle Vex – were Topunders; that is to say, magical people who can live with the ghosts in Underland, or with the Topsiders. Unfortunately, they don't fully fit in either land. They're a bit too alive for the Underlanders and a bit too mischievous for the Topsiders.

Malice turned the card over in her hand and then flicked it away. What else could she do? She couldn't be part of an investigation that might involve her parents. They were rotten as pigswill but they were still her parents. Not for the first time, Malice felt like she was trapped between wanting to do right by her parents and wanting to do what felt right in her heart. The card landed on the ground and Malice watched as it was quickly covered in a carpet of bronze leaves. She bit her lip and tried not to think about the missing grandad ghosts as she wandered home.

NOT OUR PROBLEM

When Malice arrived back at Malignant House, Ma was busy making stink-bombs in the kitchen. Coils of noxious green smoke rose from several test-tubes resting on the breadboard. Ma sang while she worked – she had the voice of a constipated banshee.

Ma was a tall, skinny woman, made taller by stiletto-heeled shoes, so high they were practically stilts. She always wore a bra that was eight sizes too big, so she could drop jewellery into it when her and Pa were out robbing. This made her dress hang rather oddly, as though she were smuggling two ferrets down her top.

"I saw Uncle Vex, in the square," said Malice. She said it almost without thinking. The case of the disappearing grandads he was working on was playing on her mind.

"You what?" asked Ma, now distracted from stink-bomb making. The tight curls around her face twisted and bounced like worms in a rugby scrum.

Malice swallowed nervously.

"I saw Uncle Vex," she continued. "He's investigating disappeared grandads." Malice studied Ma's face for signs of guilt, or knowledge of the missing ghosts. Ma's face showed nothing but its usual sourness.

"Typical!" snorted Ma. "Always poking his beak into honest skulduggery. I hope you told him to sling his hook! Fuzzy do-gooder!"

Ma's expression was that of a woman who is

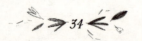

being permanently pinched. Her lips were two thin disapproving lines, smudged with red lipstick which looked as though it had been applied in a gale force wind with her eyes shut.

"He asked me to help him with the investigation," said Malice.

"Help! Malice Morbid Malign." Malice knew she was in trouble when Ma used her full name. "We look after our own kingdom. Let someone else look after the others."

"But ghosts are being disappeared!" said Malice.

"What do we care?" Ma snapped. "Not our ghosts. Not our kingdom. Not our problem."

Pa strolled in rubbing his eyes. A cloud of flies always followed Pa around, buzzing above his greasy head. Pa was a short, round man; when he stood next to Ma his head only just reached her oversized bra. Pa considered himself to be a man of business, and as such, he wore a suit, the buttons of which he

had been unable to fasten since 1972 because of his ever-expanding belly.

"What's all the racket?" he asked.

Ma rested her hands on her bony hips.

"Vex asked Malice to *help* with an investigation," said Ma.

Pa snapped into full alert. The kitchen ghosts

dived into the scullery for cover.

"Help!" roared Pa. "We do not help! This house is our castle and this family is our kingdom!"

His chest puffed in and out like a set of bellows and the buttons on his shirt strained against his stomach like a puffer fish trapped in a net. Bits of plaster shivered and dropped off the ceiling.

"That's what I told her!" said Ma indignantly.

"We didn't bring you up to HELP!" shouted Pa. His pasty face had turned a pastel blush. Unlike Ma, Pa had big wet lips like a codfish and when he was cross, they seemed to wobble of their own accord; they were wobbling now.

Ma, who delighted in whisking Pa up into a frenzy, folded her arms and sucked in her already gaunt cheeks.

"I'll bet you two shillings she was reading BOOKS this morning, while we were out mischief-making!"

"Books!" spluttered Pa. "Books! Books means

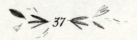

reading and reading means education and education means knowledge." He brought his voice down to a whisper. "The root of all g-g-g-good!" he shuddered. Then he threw his arms into the air and wailed: "Where? Where did we go wrong?"

"You do your worst for 'em and this is how they repay you," sobbed Ma, dabbing at her eyes with a used teabag.

"Books aren't so bad." Malice tried to reason with her parents. "Books are exciting! And I'm sure you could find all sorts of mischief in them, if you read the right ones."

"The shame of it," said Ma, teetering on her stilettos. "She hasn't even got the decency to lie!"

"This is how it starts," cried Pa. "One day it's a book, the next it's signing up for litter picking!" He shuddered. "I think I'm going to be sick!"

"Ooh, I've come over all of a fluster," moaned Ma, grabbing a cabbage leaf to fan herself with.

She looked over at Malice and snapped, "You need to go away and think about what you've done, young lady!"

"Sorry," Malice mumbled as she left the kitchen.

Malice knew her parents loved her, but they didn't understand her. She wished they did. Sometimes she felt so different to them, it was like she was an alien in her own family. She didn't fit in with the residents of Felicity Square and she didn't fit in with her family. *Where* do *I fit in?* Malice wondered.

Malice slunk along dark passages and through vast decaying rooms on her way to find Grandad. As she passed the dilapidated ballroom, she heard her sister whimpering in her sleep. Antipathy-Rose's crib was a large iron birdcage which hung from the ceiling on a long chain. The bottom of the cage was generously lined with feather pillows and soft eiderdowns embroidered with gurning gargoyles. Malice pulled a deep-fried pig's ear that she'd bought

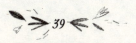

from the pet store out of her pocket and pushed it between the bars of the cage into Antipathy-Rose's hot, sticky hand. The baby stopped whimpering and settled down to gnaw on the pig's ear in her sleep.

MOTHS HAVE THE NICEST TABLE MANNERS

Malice climbed the twisted staircase to the attic. It kinked and curved at seemingly impossible angles to mirror the strange architecture of the building. Malignant House had many attic rooms, but Grandad's was nestled in the roof-space between two turrets in the west wing. The stairs narrowed here and the climb became awkward – far too awkward for Ma and Pa to bother with, which was precisely why Grandad had picked it.

To the untrained eye the attic was nothing but a dark and draughty place, piled high with old leather trunks, packing cases and discarded suits of armour. But peer through the cracks and steer through the gaps, and you would find a small clearing in the chaos: Grandad's attic hideaway.

An old tapestry rug covered the floorboards and stacks of leather-bound books made handy stands for reading lamps, which gently lit the space. Grandad reclined in a moth-eaten, wing-back armchair; his feet, in holey tartan slippers, rested on a plush velvet footstool.

"There you are, Duck!" said Grandad as Malice squeezed through a gap between two old wardrobes. "Make yourself comfy."

In front of Grandad, a table was laid out for poker and another chair, equally moth-eaten, sat opposite. Most people get annoyed when moths eat their fabrics but really, they should be honoured;

moths are very picky eaters and if they decide to eat your armchair, then it's a credit to your good taste in furniture.

The moths in Grandad's attic were particularly friendly and had been endlessly patient with Malice while she practised her moth-whispering technique. They would politely nibble the chairs – moths have the nicest table manners – and applaud when Malice perfected a spell, by rubbing their wings together and sprinkling her hair with their glitter dust.

Malice flopped down into the chair opposite Grandad and felt her worries float away. This was her happy place.

Malice handed the vintage newspaper Seth had brought to Grandad. He took it eagerly and pushed it into his armchair-tidy, along with his word puzzle books. Grandad had white spikey hair, a scruffy white beard and the kindest blue eyes you ever did see, that crinkled at the edges when he

laughed. And Grandad laughed a lot!

"Thanks, Duck," he said. "And thank Seth for me. There's something not quite ordinary about that boy. I like him!"

Every few generations a Topunder is born without the menacing-mischief gene. The Malign family tree was littered with relatives who didn't cut the mischief mustard; these unfortunates were considered boils on the bum of beastly behaviour by the rest of the family. In 1392, Magnanimous Malign was such a heinously hospitable landowner that he allowed all his tenants to keep the money they made from their crops. Ludicrous! And later, in 1590, Lady Munificence Malign turned the Malign ancestral home into an almshouse for the poor! The shame!

When Malice was born, it was clear to Grandad that she, like him, had been born without the menacing-mischief gene. She had shown no interest

in biting strangers, ripping up library books or stealing candy from other babies. Instead, she liked bedtime stories, jigsaw puzzles and VEGETABLES!

Grandad saw in his little granddaughter a kindred spirit: a child who would need a different kind of nurturing to the sort offered by Ma and Pa. And so, Grandad took Malice under his wing. He showed her a merrier way of mischief – after all, mischief was still in her blood – and introduced her to the wonderful world of books. He taught her how to be kind, even when the world isn't always kind back. Grandad had made life bearable for a girl who was a misfit in every society she encountered and Malice adored him.

Grandad rubbed his ghostly hands together and pulled his glasses out of his waistcoat pocket.

"Now then," he said, scooting his footstool out of the way and shuffling his armchair up close to the table. "Let's play some poker!"

"What are we playing
for today, Grandad?"
asked Malice.

"If you win,"
he said. "You
get my *Graveyards
Compendium*. If I win,
I get the stash of jellybeans
from under your bed."

"You can't even eat them!"
laughed Malice.

"I don't want to eat them," grinned
Grandad. "I want to flick them at Pa
when he's sleeping!"

Grandad's mischief was merry
and minor, just the way mischief should
be. Grandad was Ma's father. He was part of the
Rascally family, one of the oldest Topunder families
in Britain. Have you ever dropped a piece of paper in

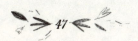

the street only to have it whisked out of your reach every time you try to pick it up? Then you've more than likely been pranked by one of the Rascally ghosts. Those times when you trip up, apparently on thin air? That'll be two Rascally ghosts holding a piece of invisible string across the path. They are for the most part, what you would call, naughty but nice.

Grandad could do all sorts of magic since he became a ghost, but when he was alive, his special gift was levitation, like Antipathy-Rose. He'd been trying to teach Malice to levitate, but so far, she seemed to be better at falling than floating.

Grandad and granddaughter settled down to play poker, using crispy dead bugs for betting chips. There were so many dead bugs in Malignant House that it seemed a waste not to use them; Malice liked to think of it as a form of recycling.

As they played, Grandad talked about "back in

the day" and Malice listened contentedly. Grandad had met a lot of interesting people during his time both dead and alive; he'd sailed on the Underland sea with Vikings, played poker with Greek philosophers and been in a book club with some ancient Egyptians (very keen on books about cats were those ancient Egyptians). Sometimes he talked about the adventures he'd had with her nana, before they'd divorced. Malice didn't get to see her nana much because she ran a spa hotel called the Weary Necromancer, in the Wild Witch Woods, so it was nice to hear about her when Grandad was in the mood to reminisce.

Nana was a witch from a long line of witches before her. Grandad said Malice and Nana were very alike; they both liked riddles and puzzles, which is a very witchy thing to like. Grandad enjoyed a good puzzle conundrum too and he and Malice enjoyed solving them together. He said they

were good for keeping the wits sharp. Grandad said as long as your heart was big and your wits were sharp, you would never go far wrong.

Grandad spent a lot of time on his own. Malice knew he was often lonely when she was at school or out making mischief, and the thought of it made her feel sad. Contrary to popular opinion, ghosts enjoyed company and they LOVED gossip. But since Ma and Pa were only good for gossip about mischief and ways to make more of it, Grandad tended to avoid their company.

Malice bet three more dead bugs, dropping them into a pile on the table.

"I think I'm having a funny turn," said Grandad.

"Are you trying to distract me so you can cheat?" Malice smiled. No one cheated better at cards than Grandad.

"Not this time, Duck," said Grandad. "I feel a bit odd. And not in a good way!"

Malice looked up from her cards. "Odd how?" she asked, a prickle of unease rising in her chest.

As she stared at him, Grandad's ghostly figure quivered blurrily, then blipped out of sight completely, then blipped back in again.

"Grandad?" said Malice, slightly panicked. "What's happening?"

"I feel like I'm being pulled away," Grandad said.

"Pulled away where?" Malice asked, her voice raised higher than she intended.

"I don't rightly know!" cried Grandad with surprise.

At that moment a pair of hands came up through the floorboards, grabbed Grandad by the ankles, yanked him off his armchair and back down through the floor.

EVEN HER TEETH
FELT TENSE

"Grandad!" shouted Malice.

Malice ran down the attic steps and burst on to the landing, in time to see Grandad's head disappear down through the hall carpet.

Malice hurtled down the stairs to the next floor, then the next, then the next. But each time she was just too late.

"Help!" Malice shouted as she ran. "Quick! Help!"

Pa swaggered out of the TV room and into the hall,

wagging his finger. "How many times must I say it, young lady? WE DO NOT HELP!"

Malice pushed passed him and made for the next set of stairs, as Grandad's arms disappeared into the floor.

"It's Grandad!" Malice cried. "He's being disappeared!"

"Whaaat?" Pa blustered.

He began to lumber after Malice, slowed down by the weight of his enormous belly.

Finally, Malice reached the cellar. Grandad was up to his waist in the stone floor. Malice launched herself across the flagstones and grabbed at Grandad's hands. But she only met with air; ghosts don't have grabbable hands.

"Grandad!" cried Malice, as Grandad slowly disappeared down into the floor. "Tell me what to do!"

"HELP!" came Grandad's disembodied voice.

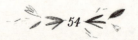

"Grandad!" Malice shouted into the floor. "Grandad?"

There was no reply. Grandad was gone.

Pa clomped down the cellar stairs, wheezing and swearing and sweating.

"Well?" he gasped. "Where is he?"

Malice shrugged her shoulders in disbelief. She didn't know what to think. Her mind was in turmoil. Who could have taken Grandad and why? And where would they take him? The questions whizzed around her head and her stomach felt sick with worry.

"I don't know," she said quietly. "He's just gone. I think he's been disappeared."

"Then you'd better appear him back again, betten you!" roared Pa.

Pa's shout was like a clap of thunder that snapped Malice out of her turbulent thoughts and dropped her firmly back into the moment. She was still frightened and confused by what had happened but her mind

was sharp and she knew what she had to do. She had to find Grandad. And she knew exactly who could help her.

Malice dashed out of the house and into the autumn sunshine. She ran to the old oak tree where she had tossed Uncle Vex's card and fumbled about in the leaves. The card was her ticket, an entry pass to Underland.

After several minutes of searching, though, Malice realized that the card had gone. Without it, she wasn't going anywhere. No one, not even a Topunder, can enter Underland without permission or invitation. The rules are there for good reason; you can't have Topsiders accidentally finding portals and dropping into Underland willy-nilly. It just wouldn't do. Right now, Malice needed to find her uncle, and her uncle would be back in Underland, investigating, and she needed to get there fast. She needed that card!

"Oh!" Malice muttered. "Help help help!"

"Looking for this?" asked Seth. He had wandered up behind her as she scrabbled around the crusty autumn spoils.

He was holding out the small black card.

"Thanks, Seth," gasped Malice. She couldn't believe her luck. "How did you know it was mine?"

Seth shrugged. "It's got your name on it," he said. "I was hoping I'd find you here. I didn't want to come up to the house; your letterbox has got teeth!"

Malice looked at the card. Sure enough, written across its shiny black surface in gold lettering were the words:

"It was a funny thing," said Seth, scratching his head. "I'd just finished my paper round over on Victoria Terrace, when a pile of leaves gusted up the street and landed by my feet. That card was sitting on top of it. The next moment a big black bird swooped down and started pecking the ground and squawking at me. It sounded like it was saying *pick-it-up, pick-it-up*. So, I did."

"Thank you, Seth!" said Malice, relief flooding through her. "I owe you one."

"Anytime," said Seth. "What's the emergency?"

"Grandad's been disappeared!" whispered Malice. She didn't know who might be listening.

Seth's mouth dropped open.

"Oh no. Poor Grandad. What are you going to do?"

"I'm going to find him and bring him back," said Malice. "Hopefully," she added.

"How would someone even disappear a ghost?" Seth asked. "And why?"

"I don't know," Malice replied. Even her teeth felt tense. "That's what I need to find out." She waggled the card. "And this is going to help me do it."

"Is there anything I can do?" asked Seth.

"Not right now, thanks," said Malice. She would dearly have liked to take Seth down to Underland with her, but only the person named on the invitation was allowed to enter the land of ghosts. "But maybe later?" she continued.

"Anytime at all!" said Seth.

"Thanks, Seth. You're the best!"

"That's what friends are for," said Seth. "Good luck!"

He smiled at her and cycled away, leaving Malice alone in Felicity Square.

Malice looked down at the card.

"'For help whisper here,'" Malice read out loud. "What does that mean? Whisper what? Whisper where?" She didn't have time for cryptic messages.

A big black bird flew down and settled
in the branches of the old oak tree just above
Malice's head.

"Do-as-you're-told!
Do-as-you're-told!
Do-as-you're-told!" the big black
bird squawked.

Malice looked from the card to the big black bird
and back again. When a bird tells you something,
you'd better be ready to listen. Birds know their stuff.

"Well," she said. "It's telling me to *whisper here*.
So here goes!"

Malice lifted the card up to her lips and very
softly whispered:

"Here!"

The old oak tree began to quiver. The tentacle
roots protruding from the base of its trunk began
to wiggle up and down like an octopus playing the
piano. It looked like the tree was getting ready to

60

uproot and walk away. As Malice wondered what that would look like, there was a loud PING! And a door-sized section of bark slid away to reveal a friendly-faced skeleton in a bellboy uniform.

"'Allo!" said the skeleton. "You whispered here?"

"Yes," said Malice. "I need to get to my uncle in Underland." Malice held out the card from Uncle Vex and the skeleton checked it over and nodded.

"Then you'd best step this way," said the skeleton.

He moved to one side and swooped down into a low, graceful bow which made all his bones clack. Malice stepped into the tree trunk and the skeleton slid the bark back across. Inside was a panel, as tall as Malice with several hundred blinking buttons and several hundred destinations scribbled next to them.

"Which uncle might you be wanting to find?"

"Uncle Vexatious Malign," said Malice. "Private Underland Investigator."

The skeleton ran a bony finger up and down the panel until he found the right name. He looked at Malice.

"Going down," he said and pressed the button. "Hold on tight!"

The lift jiggered. The lift dropped. Malice's feet swooshed off the floor from the force and she clung tightly to the handrail. The speedy descent whipped her upside-down so that her boots brushed the ceiling and her hair fell over her face.

Classical music played through a speaker in the bark and the skeleton conducted an imaginary orchestra as they fell. Suddenly the lift jolted to a stop and Malice plopped upright. She felt a little dizzy and had the sensation that her stomach was somewhere up near her brain. Her feet felt as though they were moving along a travellator.

"Here we are," grinned the skeleton. "Have a grim day!"

He pulled on a lever. The bottom of the lift dropped open and Malice hurtled out. She fell through a chalky ceiling and landed in a cloud of white dust on a squashy brown leather armchair. The bump at least seemed to put her stomach back where it ought to be.

Malice looked about her. She was in a waiting room. A low coffee table next to the sofa offered copies of the latest Underland magazines: *Haunt & Howl*, *Phantom Fashion* and *Spectre Weekly*. The walls were adorned with framed certificates from the Underland Detective University and a newspaper article from the *Daily Spook*: a grainy photograph of Uncle Vex smiling smugly beneath a headline which read, *Private Investigator Foils Zombie Tomatoes*.

Beyond the room was a door – half glass, half wood – with a plaque that read:

VEXATIOUS MALIGN
PRIVATE UNDERLAND INVESTIGATOR

Malice extricated herself from the dusty armchair and knocked on the door.

"Come in!" called Uncle Vex.

Malice pushed the door open. There was a desk with a computer and a photo frame on it, and two chairs but no sign of her uncle.

"Won't be a minute!" came Uncle Vex's voice. "Make yourself comfortable."

Malice turned the picture frame to face her; a black-and-white photograph of two boys with their arms around each-other grinned out at her: Pa and Uncle Vex. Malice smiled to herself and sat down. Aside from the desk and chairs, there was a large leather trunk with multiple padlocks, and a tall, rather battered mahogany filing cabinet with a small stepladder leaned against it, and a hatstand with a

trench coat and a fedora hat hanging from it. The room was windowless but there was a definite breeze blowing from somewhere. It seemed to be coming from the trunk.

What a strange day this was turning out to be, she thought to herself. First Grandad disappearing and then an impromptu drop-in to the land of the dead.

Malice had been born in Underland but her parents had moved Topside when she was a baby and she hadn't visited since. Nana Rascally usually came to Malignant House just before Halloween each year and so Malice had had little reason to come to Underland. Malice tried to avoid the rest of her relatives as much as possible; compared to them, Ma and Pa looked positively prim. She didn't know if she felt excited or nervous to be back. She wondered if she would feel even more of a misfit in Underland than she did up in Topside.

Malice was sure that her beloved grandad must

be down here somewhere. All the clues seemed to point to it: there were the disappeared cosy grandad ghosts for a start, and only an Underlander would have the audacity to pull a ghost down through the ground by his ankles! She had to find Grandad; he hadn't been to Underland in years. He was such a friendly ghost; what if the ghost-napper was mean? What if they had him captive in a dungeon, or an oubliette like the one Ma and Pa used for their haunting ghosts? Grandad would hate that; he liked cosy places and slippers and stinging nettle tea. Malice drummed her fingers impatiently on the desk. She didn't want to be waiting around in an office. She wanted to get out there and find Grandad!

The top drawer of the filing cabinet suddenly pushed itself open with a swish and Uncle Vex poked his head out.

"Malice! Glad you decided to come!" he said, smiling.

Malice jumped up from the chair.

"Grandad's been disappeared," she said.

Uncle Vex's smile faltered.

"Oh dear," he said, biting his lip. "Oh dear oh dear. I am most vexed to hear this."

"Who would want to disappear Grandad?" said Malice. "He's the best, kindest grandad ever! We have to find him, there's no time to lose!"

"We'd better get straight to work then!" said Uncle Vex. "Pull up that stepladder and climb on in."

Uncle Vex's head disappeared back into the open drawer. Malice did as she was told and clambered awkwardly into the filing cabinet.

Rather than seeing files and paperwork, as one might expect from the inside of an article of office furniture, Malice found herself at the top of a steep, narrow staircase. Uncle Vex stood a few steps down, smiling encouragingly at her.

The drawer behind her slid to a close with a click

and a plain blue door at the bottom of the staircase swung open, flooding the narrow stairwell in a pool of pumpkin-coloured light. Malice followed her uncle down the stairs and stood beside him at the open door.

"Ready?" he asked.

"Ready!" Malice replied. And they stepped out into Underland.

A CHRISTMAS TREE FAIRY AT A HALLOWEEN CONVENTION

Underland was made up of narrow zigzagged streets and alleyways which teemed with life – odd when you consider that most people here were dead.

Hundreds of years ago, there were Topunder families from all over the British Isles living in Underland. Topside hadn't always been the friendliest place to live if you were magical, especially if you happened to be a bit witchy in the seventeenth century.

But over time, most Topunders found they could make a better living among the living, and gradually most migrated Topside. Topsiders were ripe for pilfering, pick-pocketing and pinching from. Shrewd mischief-makers enjoyed successful careers in the whisky smuggling and highwayman business well into the eighteenth century.

Now, only a handful of alive people made their homes in Underland and Uncle Vex was one of them.

The streets of Underland were steeped in an eerie bronze glow, as though it was permanently dusk. Malice looked up. High above, the sky was a ceiling of chocolate-brown earth, alive with a mass of twisting tree roots, twining and weaving and dangling down like tangled witch's hair. In amongst the roots, millions of tiny glow-worms wriggled around, pulsing out light to brighten the darkness.

Old-fashioned lamp posts dotted the streets

below and added their gentle yellow candlelight to the glow-worm sky. The air was noisy with the sound of rickety carriage wheels on cobblestones, street sellers calling out their wares and ghostly horses whinnying impatiently as they waited for their next fare. A range of smells washed over Malice, not all of them nice but most of them familiar – she did live with Pa, after all.

"Now then," said Uncle Vex. "Please explain to me how Grandad's disappearance came about."

"We were playing poker," Malice began.

"Who was winning?"

"Does it matter?"

"No. I was just curious. Do go on."

Malice began again.

"We were playing poker, when Grandad began to feel strange and then a pair of hands came up through the floor and pulled Grandad down through it."

Uncle Vex pulled a pencil from his pocket and

chewed it thoughtfully.

"From the ghost-witness accounts I've gathered at the scenes, all the grandads have been disappeared in the same fashion," he said.

"And is it only grandads who are being disappeared?" Malice asked.

"Yes," Uncle Vex replied. "It's a right knotty case. How do you suggest we begin to unravel it?"

"You're asking me?" said Malice. "You're the investigator!"

"Yes," Uncle Vex mused, rubbing his chin. "I'm the investigator. And I'm flummoxed. Which is why I need some fresh eyes on the case – that's you."

"All right. What leads have you found so far?" Malice asked, feeling a little frustrated. "What have you detected?"

Uncle Vex looked a little vexed.

"Well, I've looked in all the places grandads usually like to hang out: parks, chiropodists, garden

centres… I've also spoken to my informants in the, shall we say, shadier districts.

"And?" Malice asked.

"No luck I'm afraid. None of them had gotten wind of a grandad heist in the pipeline. The Cosy Grandad's Agency said each of the grandads clocked in at his Topside residence for sweet-dream duty and never clocked out. Over the last forty-eight hours every cosy grandad from the Cosy Grandad's Agency has been disappeared. And no one has seen pipe nor slippers of them since. What with your grandad now being disappeared, it looks as though the ghost-nappers aren't only targeting the Cosy Grandads Agency."

This was not what Malice wanted to hear. No clues at all? How could a gaggle of grandads simply disappear into thin air? Malice looked about her. The streets were heaving with ghosts going about their daily business. Ladies with large hats bustled past, the hems of their long dresses dragging in the wet mud. Men with walking canes and pocket watches blustered by importantly. Some gave Malice sideways stares, but when they saw she was with Uncle Vex they carried on their way. Malice thought about Grandad, worried and lonely and her heart squeezed. With a fresh determination she steadied her nerve.

"How would a ghost normally arrive in Underland?" Malice asked.

"By the Ghost Express," answered Uncle Vex. He pointed to a sign which read "Underland Central Station".

"Then that's where we'll start," said Malice determinedly.

The station wasn't far, though it took them a little while to negotiate their way through the crowded streets.

In Topside, ghosts are wispy and easy to walk through because they are only visitors to the land of the living. The stuff ghosts are made of doesn't translate when they cross the boundary between worlds.

However, in Underland, ghosts are fully formed and solid. Try and walk through a ghost in Underland and you'll wish you hadn't. Similar rules apply in reverse for Topsiders in Underland; Malice's form remained solid in the land of the dead because she was a Topunder, but she still stuck out like a Christmas tree fairy at a Halloween convention.

So, it was with due care and attention that the duo slowly dodged and swerved and made "excuse me"s through the eerie streets.

Underland Central Station was chaotic. Porters pushed teetering trunks on trolleys and guards bustled and blew their whistles. Giant steam engines rolled in and out of the station like armoured beetles, pulling snaking lines of wooden carriages behind them.

Malice and Uncle Vex fought their way past ghostly travellers and through the thick smoke which billowed out from the engines and rolled along the platform like grey candyfloss.

They found a guard ticking names off a clipboard, as ghosts embarked and disembarked a train with the name *Deadly Belle* painted in a cheery yellow along the carriages.

"Excuse me," said Malice to the guard.

The guard didn't look up from his clipboard.

"Next stop is Wild Witch Woods," he barked. "The train leaves in five minutes."

"Thank you," said Malice. "But I don't want to catch a train."

"Don't want to catch a train!" snapped the guard. "What are you doing in a train station if you don't want to catch a train?"

"I was hoping to ask you some questions about missing ghosts," said Malice sweetly.

"Missing!" The guard's moustache bristled above his top lip like a million millipede legs doing a dance. "Ghosts do not go *missing* on my watch. I have a clipboard! I can account for every ghost that arrives and departs from this here station!"

Malice nodded.

"That's what I told my Uncle Vex here," said Malice. "I told him, there's only one ghost in the *whole* Under-rail network who can be relied upon to know the arrival and departure of every ghost. And that ghost is," Malice quickly read the guard's name badge, "Rod Piston, rail guard extraordinaire!"

The guard pulled his shoulders back and jutted out his chin and chest simultaneously.

"How very kind of you to say so," Rod Piston said. "It's nice to know one's efforts don't go unnoticed." He paused and then asked, "Your Uncle Vex wouldn't be Vexatious Malign, would he?"

"Why, yes," said Uncle Vex, smoothly. He stepped forward and held out his hand. "I am the very man!"

Rod Piston sucked air in between his teeth and made a hissing noise.

"You want to be careful, young miss," he said to Malice. "I was on duty the day his last apprentice boarded a runaway ghost train never to be seen again."

Malice looked at her uncle. Uncle Vex let his hand drop to his side. His face took on a sheepish expression.

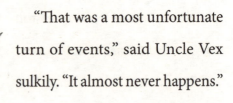

"That was a most unfortunate turn of events," said Uncle Vex sulkily. "It almost never happens."

"I suggest you be more careful with your charges in the future," advised Rod Piston.

Uncle Vex looked at the ground and took a step back, pulling out his notebook and pencil and looking concentratedly at his notes. Rod Piston addressed Malice: "Missing ghosts, you say?"

"Yes, sir," Malice said. "We are trying to locate some disappeared grandads and we wondered if any might have come in on the Ghost Express?"

Rod Piston scratched his chin as he pondered.

"None," he said firmly. "I would know if there was a sudden influx of grandads. But now that you mention it," he went on, "you're not the first people to be asking about grandads."

"We're not?" asked Uncle Vex.

Malice's heart caught in her throat. *A clue!* she thought to herself. *A clue that could lead me closer to finding Grandad!*

"No indeed," said Rod Piston. "Just the other day a

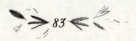

young lady came around asking if anyone had seen her grandad."

"Did she tell you her name?" asked Malice.

"Nope," said Rod Piston. "And I didn't ask. The only names I'm interested in are the ones on my clipboard."

"Can you remember what she looked like?" Malice asked.

"Nope," said Rod Piston. "The only faces I remember are those whose names are on my clipboard."

Malice tapped her foot impatiently, her hopes were fizzing away like a deflating balloon.

"Can you tell us anything at all about her?" Malice asked desperately.

Rod Piston shaped his mouth to say *nope* and then frowned.

"There was one thing," he said.

"Yes?" enquired Malice hopefully.

"She smelled ever so strongly of burnt chestnuts!"

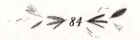

Malice couldn't hide her disappointment; that did not seem like it would be very helpful. At that moment another ghost train pulled into the station and Rod Piston sprang away from Malice and Uncle Vex, clipboard ready to check off the new arrivals.

Malice and Uncle Vex walked back through the station. There were posters on the walls advertising holiday destinations with catchy slogans such as: "Visit Wild Witch Woods, If You Dare!" and "Terror Island – Sorcery, Sand and Squalling Storms!"

And in amongst these, smaller and without pictures, Malice noticed an advert which read:

TIRED OF THE GHOSTLY GRIND?

Want to terrify and terrorize nice Topside families?

WAIT NO LONGER!

Visit the

MALIGN HAUNTING AGENCY

today

and make your nightmares
COME TRUE!

It was an advertisement for her parents' haunting business. Malice always experienced a sinking feeling when she thought about her family's line of work; it was so thoroughly unpleasant. "I suppose we'd better check the agency out," she said. "Just to be sure my parents don't have their sticky hands in this disappearing grandad business."

Uncle Vex nodded and pulled a sympathetic face.

"Although it seems unlikely that they would be in on a caper that involved disappearing *our* grandad," said Malice and she laughed uncertainly. "I mean, they enjoy a dastardly deed as much as the next Topunder, but ghost-napping members of your own family is a bit much, even for them."

Uncle Vex raised his eyebrows and began to whistle in a way that suggested he wouldn't like to comment.

"Come on then," Malice sighed. "Let's get this over with."

"This way," said Uncle Vex gently and he led Malice away from Underland Central Station and towards the murky alleyways of the Haunting Quarter, where Ma and Pa had their office. Malice was confident her parents wouldn't be there; they could rarely be bothered to make the journey down to Underland. Instead, they hired agents to run the Underland office for them, while they took care of the Topside portion of the business: seeking out nice houses to haunt and interviewing potential haunters in the oubliette.

OUT SNEAK THE SNEAKERS

The Haunting Quarter was not a friendly place to visit. The streets were dark and so narrow you had to walk in single file. It was quieter than the rest of Underland, too. There were no street hawkers calling in sing-voices, no horse-drawn carriages clattering glamourous ghosts to afternoon teas, or portly police ghosts blowing their whistles and chasing chimney sweeps. Instead, the air was heavy with mistrust and dodgy dealings. The sounds here were the echoing drip drip drips of water down

slippery walls, the swoosh of hooded capes, and the soft footsteps of nefarious phantoms hurrying past in the gloom.

This area attracted the more ghoulish ghouls. If you wanted the ingredients for a horrendous hex or a cruel curse or just a nasty case of the pox, the Haunting Quarter was where you would find them.

"Keep close," said Uncle Vex, crouching nervously behind Malice.

Of the two brothers, Uncle Vex had definitely inherited more brains than Pa, but it seemed to Malice, as her uncle tiptoed behind in her shadow, not so much of the courage. His oh-so-shiny shoes creaked and Malice thought she could hear his teeth chattering.

Shadows flitted like bats, disappearing around corners and darting into darkened doorways. Malice felt a flutter of fear but she kept her wits about her. She knew these kinds of ghosts well enough. It was ghosts just like these that her parents employed to haunt Topsiders.

Uncle Vex stopped outside a dilapidated building, whose sign read:

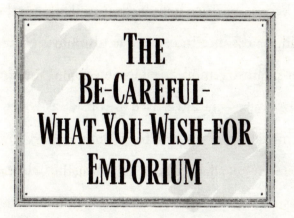

THE BE-CAREFUL-WHAT-YOU-WISH-FOR EMPORIUM

At the side of the building was a door which led upstairs to the Malign Haunting Agency's office.

Uncle Vex and Malice climbed a dingy staircase with sticky carpet. Slime dripped down the walls.

"I'll wait out here and act as lookout," said Uncle Vex when they reached the door to the office. "I'm not

very popular with the Haunting Agency."

Uncle Vex had a reputation for removing Ma and Pa's ghosts from their haunting posts and delivering them back to Underland. Sometimes he was hired by a wayward ghost's family – or the Underland police – to bring them back into the Underland fold. And sometimes he was hired by desperate Topsiders to remove troublesome apparitions from their houses – he advertised in Topside as a Spectral Removal Service. Quite often though, he did it for no money at all, because frightening the public just wasn't cricket!

"Now remember," he went on, "your parents employ the sneakiest of ghosts. The only way to get information is to out-sneak them."

"Got it," said Malice. "Out-sneak the sneakers!"

Malice pushed open the door and entered the office, which was thick with a pungent stink of feet. Photographs of nice Topside houses lined the walls,

some with stickers which read "Haunted" across them and others with "To Haunt".

A bored-looking gentleman, wearing a frock coat, and a red cravat with a tombstone tie-pin, sat with his bare foot on the desk, painting his toenails with emerald-green glitter varnish. Malice recognized him from the annual Halloween Ball at Malignant House. He looked up when Malice entered.

"What is it?" he snapped.

Malice pulled her courage around her and stepped forward.

"I'm Malice Malign," she said, in the haughtiest voice she could muster.

The receptionist put his nail varnish down and sat up straight, leaving his foot on the desk, toes wiggling.

"Oh!" he blustered. "Miss Malign! I didn't recognize you. How are your parents? Miserable I hope?" He had a nasal voice, which made everything he said sound like a sneer.

"They are despicable," Malice replied. "Thank you for asking."

The receptionist relaxed a little and Malice got to sneaking.

"My parents sent me down here to check on their Disappearing Cosy Grandads Caper," said Malice. "D.C.G.C for short," she added mischievously.

She watched the receptionist's expression turn from surprise to confusion to panic.

"Disappearing grandads?" the receptionist yelped. "A cosy caper, you say? Was there a memo? I don't remember getting a memo!"

He began to riffle through the papers on his desk. A poster on his wall caught Malice's eye; it was a portrait of Uncle Vex with a headline which read "Beware! Goody-Do-Gooder!"

"I can assure you," the receptionist gabbled, "that if I'd *had* a memo, it would have been my greatest pleasure to assist in the disappearing of those pesky cosy grandads – always getting in the way of a good haunting! But I've had nothing of the sort."

Malice felt relieved. *Maybe Ma and Pa aren't in on this dastardly deed*, she thought.

"Never mind. The memo must have got lost in the ghost-post," Malice lied. "I'll get Ma to send another one."

Malice wasn't a good liar, but the receptionist seemed to believe her story. She watched the toes on his foot droop with relief.

She was about to leave, when she remembered how much ghosts love to gossip. She arched an eyebrow.

"But you must have heard *something* about the disappearing grandads, given all the rumours," Malice goaded.

"Ah," said the receptionist. "I said *I* haven't been asked to disappear any. Not that I haven't heard rumours."

Malice grinned. "I thought to myself when I came in, *he looks like the type of ghost who knows a thing or two!* Tell me everything."

The receptionist looked pleased and leaned across the table conspiratorially. Malice leaned in as far

as she dared; the receptionist's foot smelled like a ripe stilton.

"There was a kerfuffle outside the witches wish shop downstairs," said the receptionist.

"Go on," said Malice.

"A lady. Unhappy customer. Said she'd paid for a wish and it hadn't worked," he went on. "Said she had a house full of grandads and not one of them was hers!"

Malice's heart began to race.

"When was this?" she asked urgently.

"I don't know," drawled the receptionist. "One day is much like the next. Could have been yesterday. Could have been last week."

Malice had to breathe deeply to stop herself from shaking the receptionist by his velvet lapels.

"What happened then?" she asked as calmly as she could.

"She wanted her wish reversed but the shop-

witches said no," said the man. "And then she threatened to plant fresh flowers in their garden if they didn't help her! Fresh flowers!" He shuddered. "I know she was upset, but there's no need for that."

"Could you describe her to me?" Malice asked.

"I didn't get a good look at her," said the receptionist. "I was up here in the office, working hard." He looked pointedly at Malice. "So, all I could see from my window was a black hat, a black cloak and a lot of angry arm waving."

Malice sighed. That description matched half the residents of Underland.

"Didn't she have *any* distinguishing features?" asked Malice.

The receptionist screwed his face up in concentration.

"Oh," he said. "Well there was… I think she… she might have had… NO," he conceded finally. "None at all."

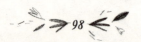

Malice thanked the receptionist and left him to his toenail varnish.

"I don't think Ma and Pa are involved," said Malice as she and Uncle Vex descended the stairs. "The receptionist didn't know anything about it. But he did hear a woman arguing with the witches in the shop below. Something about grandads. That's worth checking out."

Uncle Vex scratched his chin.

"So, your parents are off the hook. Unless," he pondered, "you tried to out-sneak the sneaker but the sneaker caught a whiff of your out-sneaking and out-sneaky-sneakered you! What do you say to that?"

Malice rolled her eyes.

"I say we pay a visit to the Be-Careful-What-You-Wish-For Emporium," said Malice.

WITCHES ARE WEAVERS
OF WORDS

The Be-Careful-What-You-Wish-For Emporium was stacked to the ceiling with glass vials of all shapes and sizes. Each vial held a wish and each wish was a different colour depending on its potency and type. Shades of green for envious wishes, blood-red for wishes of the heart and black for wishes of revenge. The wishes glooped lazily in the vials, like lava-lamps.

The smell in the shop was familiar; it reminded Malice of the base ingredients for Ma's stink-bomb

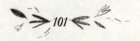

spell. Rotten eggs, decomposing fish skin and rancid milk. It was one of those stinks that is so strong, it coats the inside of your nostrils and your tongue with a kind of chalky fur.

"Is this where Ma buys her perfume from?" Uncle Vex asked.

A ghoul with its face shrouded by a cloak brushed passed them, clutching a black bubbling vial. Uncle Vex gulped and motioned for Malice to walk ahead of him.

"You go ahead and I'll, ah, keep watch from behind your shoulder," he whispered.

They walked gingerly between the tall teetering aisles, Uncle Vex shambling along in a crouch behind Malice. The wishes in the vials whispered to them in viperous tones, cajoling and enticing them with empty promises and vicious threats. The ampoules glowed brighter as Malice and Uncle Vex passed by them, clinking together ever so slightly, so that the emporium was alive with a tinkling sound like wind chimes.

At the back of the emporium, visible between two red linen drapes pulled back like curtains in a theatre, three wizened shop-witches were taking turns to stir a putrid purple concoction in a giant cauldron. Their thick black hair was varying degrees of wild, from scarecrow to Mongolian Yak to Medusa. Each witch wore a long black tea gown, with big puffy sleeves and stains in various colours dribbled down their lace bib collars. Malice approached cautiously, so as not to startle them. Uncle Vex stayed close behind her, the pencil in his hand shaking as he held it poised to make notes in his notebook.

The shop-witches looked up and grinned toothlessly.

"Here she is!" exclaimed one.

"We've been expecting you," sniggered another.

"Our paths are bound to cross and cross again," promised the last witch.

"That's nice," said Malice. Malice wasn't afraid of witches; after all she was part witch herself. Witches like these – that is to say, your classic crones: wise women of unkempt appearance and scientific mind – were vastly misunderstood. For the most part they were all warts and no wicked, although you'd be wise not to upset them, just in case.

"How did you know I was coming?" asked Malice.

"By the pricking of our thumbs," said the first witch.

"Malice Morbid this way comes," said the second.

"Then you'll know why I'm here," Malice said. "I'm searching for my grandad. He was disappeared and I believe he is here in Underland. I think you may have information that could help me find him."

The shop-witches glowered at Malice from beneath hairy caterpillar eyebrows.

"He's not in *this* shop," said the first witch.

"And if he's not in *this* shop…" said the second witch.

"Then he's not *our* problem!" finished the third.

Malice was used to this kind of attitude. "Not our problem" was practically the Malign family motto.

"Actually, I'm interested in one of your customers. A lady who wasn't happy with the wish she purchased here, in *this* shop," said Malice.

"That doesn't narrow it down much," cackled the third witch.

"She should have read the small print," tutted the first witch.

"The devil is in the detail," warned the second.

The third witch pointed to a sign on the wall with tiny writing. Malice screwed her eyes up and read the small print:

Wishes brewed with pulp and dread,

Granting nightmares for the dead.

Seek the things you want the most,

Treasures for the desperate ghost.

Beware, one wish can lead to more,

Take care with what you're wishing for.

Malice realized she was going to have to be specific; these witches were wilier than most and, she suspected, excellent at avoiding questions concerning their business practices. "Can you tell me anything about the lady who bought the grandad wish?"

"No," said the first witch.

"Why not?" asked Malice.

"Data protection," said the second.

Malice looked at her uncle with raised eyebrows. Uncle Vex looked up from his notebook.

"Ghosts have a right to privacy too, you know," he said.

"But a lady *did* buy a wish from *this* shop, regarding one or more grandads," Malice cajoled, trying to get the witches to confirm something.

"We ain't saying there was such a lady, nor such a wish," sniffed the second witch.

"But we ain't saying there wasn't, neither," said the first shrewishly.

"You must understand that client confidentiality is very important for a small business such as ours," the third crone crooned.

Malice considered the situation. These witches were not going to be persuaded by reason or pleading or even threats. Not that she had anything to threaten them with, and her uncle would be of no use in this department – he hadn't stopped quivering like a blancmange since they'd arrived. As Grandad would say, she was going to have to use her wits. She decided to appeal to their witchy nature.

"OK then," Malice said. "How about if you set me a

riddle that might help me identify the lady who may or may not have bought a grandad wish?"

Malice knew that witches loved setting riddles. Riddles were the quickest way to their shrivelled hearts. Witches are weavers of words. And thanks to Grandad, Malice was very good at unpicking them.

The witches huddled in the corner and spoke in hissy-whispers. Despite their fearsome looks, Malice was convinced it would only take a good hairbrush and a trip to the dentist to have these witches looking as friendly as any Topside nana.

The long wooden spoons continued to stir the burbling brew without the aid of the witches' wrinkly hands and stopped only when their malodorous mistresses floated back to their positions around the bubbling pot.

"All right," said the first witch. "Solve this puzzle and you will have your clue."

The three witches stirred the cauldron faster and faster, the gooey mixture swirling and sloshing as they chanted:

Twinkle, twinkle diamond ring.
Spades for digging. Lonely king.
Hearts and flowers to show you care,
Leave their heads on if you dare.
Chestnuts stirred with iron poker.
Join the club, invite the joker.
Jack is ace, he's very nimble.
Your answer is the missing symbol.

The shop witches' cackles filled the air and the clink of the wish vials seemed to get louder and louder. Uncle Vex covered his ears. A breeze blew up around Malice and her uncle, whipping Malice's hair around her face and bending Uncle Vex's quiff at a most peculiar angle. Malice steadied herself against the growing gale by grasping the sides of the cauldron, Uncle Vex held tight to a shelf of jangling vials, and all the time the witches' screechy laughter grew in volume.

Malice gasped as a purple tidal wave of smoke careered down the aisle nearest them. It swept them up in a tumble of boots and flailing limbs and, in another moment, Malice and Uncle Vex found themselves unceremoniously disappeared from the Be-Careful-What-You-Wish-For Emporium, and reappeared in a dingy street in the Haunting Quarter.

"I guess we outstayed our welcome!" said Uncle Vex, brushing down his jacket.

"I guess so," agreed Malice.

But as the purple smoke ebbed away, the witches' voices whispered: "We'll be seeing you again, Malice Morbid Malign!"

Uncle Vex shuddered. Malice grinned. She had rather liked the wily witches.

"Does the puzzle mean anything to you?" he asked, smoothing his quiff.

Malice scratched her head. She could feel the answer floating at the edges of her brain, just out of her reach. She tapped her chin with her finger and her foot on the cobbles as she tried to snag the answer.

"Hmmmm," she said. "Not yet. But I'm working on it."

A POT OF STINGING NETTLE TEA

They had been reappeared nearby Uncle Vex's favourite tearooms, the Vengeful Brew, so they decided to take a quick break from investigating and stop in for a pot of tea and a scone.

"One can't possibly investigate when one is hungry," said Uncle Vex. "Feed the stomach, fuel the brain!"

Malice reluctantly agreed. She'd had nothing to eat since her bowl of cocoa-cockroaches that morning,

and although it was difficult to tell what time of day it was in Underland, she knew it must be way past lunchtime. There was a gnawing sensation in her stomach, but she didn't know if it was hunger or worry.

Malice and Uncle Vex settled themselves at a round table for two, covered in a black lace tablecloth.

The table was set for tea, but the vase beside the sugar pot was empty of flowers. Glum-faced ghouls and ghosts sat at the tables, gloomily groaning their woes. Candles flickered in black chandeliers, picking out the maniacal expressions of the villainous lords and vile ladies in the paintings on the walls, glowering out from ebony frames. Gold and black tapestry curtains adorned the sooty windows.

A ghost glided over. She wore a long evening gown of crushed silk that trailed along the floor behind her.

"Hello, Vexatious," she purred, smiling. Her teeth glinted white and her long red hair fell down to her waist in bouncy curls, decorated with silver spider hairclips.

"Hello, Belladonna," said Uncle Vex. "I'd like you meet my niece, Malice. Malice, this is my good friend Belladonna. She owns this tearoom."

Belladonna stretched out a long, slender hand for Malice to shake. Her hand was cool and smooth like

marble and her fingernails were sharp as an eagle's talons. Malice liked her instantly.

"Did your uncle tell you how he spectacularly lost his last apprentice to the elves in the Wild Witch Woods?" Belladonna asked Malice. She had a strong French accent. Malice noted something like admiration in her voice; it must have been an impressive vanishing.

"He didn't mention it," said Malice.

"That was a most unfortunate turn of events," Uncle Vex blustered. "It almost never happens!"

"Ah, those elves," Belladonna said fondly. "Such spritely scoundrels. And what brings you to the Haunting Quarter today?"

"We're investigating a case of disappeared grandads," said Uncle Vex.

"We've just come from the Be-Careful-What-You-Wish-For Emporium," said Malice.

Belladonna arched a perfect eyebrow.

"I hope you didn't buy any wishes," she said. "My customers have been less than happy with their purchases from that shop."

Belladonna pointed to a forlorn woman in a black bonnet, who was stroking a snoring hare on her lap. The hare's long ears flopped over the woman's lap and on to the carpet. Its considerable back legs draped down under the table.

Belladonna addressed the woman.

"Mrs Dismal," she called across the tearooms. "Can you please tell my friends here what you wished for in the Be-Careful-What-You-Wish-For Emporium?"

Mrs Dismal looked over to Malice and Uncle Vex, still stroking the sleeping hare.

"Long, luscious hair!" answered Mrs Dismal, dismally.

Malice stifled a laugh by burying her face in the menu. Belladonna nodded at an angry-looking baby, dripping in jewels, sitting in a highchair.

"That is Dame Vain," said Belladonna. "She wished for eternal youth!"

Uncle Vex ducked as Dame Vain hurled a rattle in his direction. The missile breezed over the top of his quiff and smacked the pirate on the table behind, right in the eyepatch. The pirate shook his fist at the baby and shouted:

"AAARRRGGHHH!"

"What can I get for you?" asked Belladonna, ignoring the commotion.

"I'll have a curdled cream tea please, Belladonna," said Uncle Vex. "With extra poison-berry jam."

The thought of curdled cream made Malice's stomach growl and she realized she must be hungry after all.

"That sounds good," said Malice. "I'll have the same, please."

Belladonna wrote down the order.

"And a pot of stinging nettle tea," added Uncle Vex.

"Stinging nettle tea is off the menu, I'm afraid," said Belladonna. "A parlour boy came in yesterday and bought our entire stock!"

"Thirsty, was he?" asked Uncle Vex.

Belladonna smiled enigmatically.

Malice let out a sigh; stinging nettle tea was her grandad's favourite. She missed him so much, it was like a permanent nagging stomach-ache.

"Hmm," mused Uncle Vex. "I'll have sewer sludge tea instead then please."

"And for you, Malice?" Belladonna's pen hovered above her pad.

"What other tea have you got?" asked Malice.

Belladonna reeled off a list:

"Deadly nightshade, foxglove, wolfsbane or dung beetle," she said.

The first three options were poisonous to the living, so Malice asked:

"Are there actual beetles in the dung beetle tea?"

"No!" chuckled Belladonna. "But there is dung."

"I'll have a water, please," said Malice.

Belladonna went off. Their tea arrived and Uncle Vex spread a large glob of curdled cream over his scone.

"So," he began, "what are our leads so far?"

"Not many," said Malice, shovelling in a mouthful of the cake. "The lady who was at Central Station is one. She could be like me, trying to find her disappeared grandad. Even if we find her, she might not know any more than we do."

Uncle Vex nodded in agreement.

"And the lady who bought the wish. Might be the same lady who spoke to Rod Piston, or another lady with grandad issues."

"Precisely," said Malice. "Although…"

Malice tapped her chin with her finger and tapped her foot beneath the table as she pondered.

"I think we need to concentrate our efforts on the

120

lady who bought the wish," said Malice.

"Why?" asked Uncle Vex.

"Because she said she had ended up with a house full of grandads, none of them hers. And it seems too much of a coincidence for someone to be complaining about having a multitude of grandads at a time when grandads are decidedly thin on the ground."

"What about the lady from the station?"

"Just for now, let's assume they are one and the same," said Malice. Uncle Vex nodded his agreement. "Now," she went on, "let's assume she bought the wish intending to wish for just *one* grandad, namely hers…"

Malice cast glances at Dame Vain and Mrs Dismal. Both women had fallen foul of the Be-Careful-What-You-Wish-For Emporium's wishes: wishes that promised one thing and delivered quite another. Malice sat up straight, her green eyes gleaming in the candlelight.

"Suppose," she said excitedly, "suppose that the disappearing grandads is *accidental*. What if we aren't looking at a case of grandad-napping at all but an unintended side-effect of a wish that went wrong."

Uncle Vex paused with a scone midway to his mouth and eyed Malice from beneath furrowed brows, nodding encouragingly as he picked up on her chain of reasoning.

"We know for a fact that the witches wishes are unreliable," Malice explained. "Now, let's imagine that the lady in question bought a wish and wished her grandad back from wherever he'd gone to…"

"Why do we think her grandad was missing in the first place?" asked Uncle Vex.

"That doesn't matter at the moment," said Malice. "The point is, he *was* missing and the lady tried to wish him back. But the wish didn't work as she'd expected. And instead of one grandad she ended up with a whole bevy of them. They weren't disappeared

by a ghostnapper at all – they were summoned by a wayward wish!"

"Though not all at the same time," added Uncle Vex. "They appear to have been disappeared one by one over the last couple of days. Any hypotheses as to why that might be?"

Malice chewed her lip as she mulled it over.

"Maybe, the longer her grandad is missing, the more grandads will land in his place?"

"A fair assumption. Which makes this a time-sensitive case," said Uncle Vex. "One can only fit so many grandads into a house before it starts to get stuffy. And where, I wonder, in all this is the woman's own grandad?"

"I don't know," replied Malice. "But I think we've figured out why she made her complaint to the witches at the emporium."

"Interesting theory!" Uncle Vex exclaimed. "And if you are right, it is imperative that we find that woman.

Have you had any luck with the witches' riddle yet?"

Malice pulled a face.

"It's so frustrating!" she said. "The answer is right there, floating around my brain like a missing jigsaw piece, but I just can't seem to catch a hold of it."

Malice wished Seth or Grandad were here so they could mull it over together. A problem was always less of a problem with a friend.

"It'll click into place," said Uncle Vex soothingly. "These things always do."

"What do we do in the meantime?" asked Malice. "How do we ever begin to find the wish customer?"

"We head to the place where the ghosts gabble and gossip like geese," said Uncle Vex.

"And where is that?" Malice asked.

"The Underland Market!" said Uncle Vex.

NO TIME FOR REVELLING IN SMUGNESS

The Underland Market had a completely different atmosphere to the Haunting Quarter. There was a feeling of high-jinx and boisterousness in the air which lifted the spirits and made you feel glad to be alive, or dead. The streets were still slippery and mud-slicked. But where the Haunting Quarter had been all lurking shadows and secret whispers, here there was noise and bustle, and the jolly sing-song chorus of the ghostly street sellers shouting about their wares…

"Get your rotten fish guts 'ere!"

And:

"Road-kill! Come and get your maggoty road-kill!"

Even the glow-worms slipping in and out of the tangled roots in the sky above seemed to glow brighter here. Grandad had often regaled Malice with stories of spectacular early worm-rises above the skanky city and glorious worm-sets over the odorous ocean. She felt sad that he wasn't with her now, so they could enjoy this worm-ridden sky together.

Malice and Uncle Vex weaved between the market stalls. Skull-and-crossbones bunting flapped merrily and a monkey grinded an organ while a skeleton danced on top of it.

Some stallholders waved at Uncle Vex and threw cautious glances at Malice. Others smiled shiftily and slid things they didn't want Uncle Vex to see under their tables. The market place was rife with slightly dodgy deals. It was all honest jiggery-pokery but

some traders were suspicious of a private detective who had helped the Underland Police with their trickier cases. Underlanders loved to moan about do-gooders. But when they found themselves the recipients of some diabolicality, it was those very do-gooders they turned to for help; Uncle Vex helped keep the nonsense from sliding into the nefarious.

They stopped at a baker's stall.

"Mouldy bread!" shouted the baker gruffly. "I've got green mould, black speckled mould, and white furry mould! The mouldiest bread in all of Underland!"

"Hi, Vex!" said the baker. "Who's this?" he added, nodding his head towards Malice.

"This is my niece, Malice," replied Uncle Vex. "She's helping me with a case."

"What kinda case?" asked the baker, narrowing his eyes.

"We're looking for disappeared ghosts," said

Malice. "Disappeared grandads to be precise."

The baker brightened.

"A ghost-napping case, is it? Well, why didn't you say so! Any friend of Vex's is a friend of mine. How can I be of service?" he asked, picking a ball of yellow wax from his ear and wiping it on a baguette.

"Have you noticed anything unusual?" asked Uncle Vex. "Anyone gone missing? Or a sudden influx of new ghosts?"

"Nuffink!" said the baker. "No one and nuffink! And nuffink gets past me, I can tell ya."

Malice looked along the rows of market stalls that lined the alley. Something caught her attention. Halfway down, a cloud of black smoke was billowing out from a burnt chestnut stall. The chestnut seller stirred the singeing nuts with a long iron poker. A breeze blew the smoke away, and as it did, another stall by the side of it came into view. It was an unmanned stall with a sign which read:

Stagnant stems

Malice frowned. The riddle flickered to the front of her mind.

Hearts and flowers to show you care,
Leave their heads on if you dare.
Chestnuts stirred with iron poker.

"Whose stall is that?" asked Malice.

"That's Queenie Florus's stall," said the baker. "She's off sick with the ghost-chills."

Malice looked at Queenie's stall. Buckets full of drooping, mildewing stalks littered the ground.

"Why are there no flowers on the stems?" Malice asked.

"She chops their heads off, don't she!" said the baker.

"Who wants fresh flowers stinking up their houses?" He shuddered at the thought.

The cogs in Malice's mind began to whirr; the jigsaw pieces that had been floating so tantalizingly just out of her reach began to shift and lock into place. Uncle Vex and the baker's voices melded into the background until they became merely another humming in the hubbub around her. Malice concentrated on the riddle and unstitched the witch's woven words, and as she did Malice felt a tingle of excitement.

1: Rod Piston had told her that the woman asking about her grandad had smelled like burnt chestnuts. There were chestnuts in the riddle. And here was a burnt chestnut stall, stirred by a chestnut seller with an iron poker. And what should be right beside it but Queenie Florus's stall.

That made Queenie a definite contender for the woman at Central Station.

2: The foul-footed receptionist at the Malign Haunting Agency had witnessed an unhappy customer threatening to plant fresh flowers in the shop-witches garden; *Leave their heads on if you dare*, said the riddle. And here was a flower seller.

Coincidence? Malice thought not. She was willing to bet a whole stack of dead bugs that Queenie Florus was also the woman seen complaining outside the Be-Careful-What-You-Wish-For Emporium.

Malice pulled the words of the shop-witches poem to the front of her mind:

Twinkle, twinkle DIAMOND ring.
SPADES for digging. Lonely KING.
HEARTS and FLOWERS to show you care,
Leave their heads on if you dare.

CHESTNUTS stirred with iron POKER.

Join the CLUB, invite the JOKER.

JACK is ACE, he's very nimble.

Your answer is the missing symbol.

Then she picked the poem apart:

Diamonds. Spades. Kings. Hearts. Clubs. Jokers. Jacks. Aces.

Those were all symbols found in a deck of cards. A poker was being used to stir the chestnuts; poker was also the name of her grandad's favourite card game.

Your answer is the missing symbol.

Malice went over the symbols in the poem again … one thing was missing. *Queens!* The missing card from the deck was the Queen. Or Queenie.

"It's the same lady!" Malice blurted. The tingle of excitement had become a firework party in her stomach. She was closer to finding Grandad.

Uncle Vex and the baker stopped their conversation and looked at Malice.

"Queenie Florus," said Malice. "The lady who smelled of burnt chestnuts at the train station and the lady who bought the wish is Queenie Florus the flower seller."

"Are you quite sure?" asked Uncle Vex.

"Absolutely!" said Malice. "It's just as I suspected; Queenie's wish went wrong, like Dame Vain and Mrs Dismal's, and she ended up with all the grandads."

Malice turned to the baker.

"I need you tell me when you last saw Queenie Florus," she said.

The urgency in her voice caused the baker to jump to attention. He scratched his head with a cheese-topped bap while he thought.

"Well," he began. "It was a regular mystery. Queenie and her grandad always work the stall together. Then one day last week, she comes tearing through the

market crying that he's been disappeared!"

"Disappeared!" repeated Malice. "I knew it!"

Uncle Vex was writing down everything the baker said in his notebook.

"What happened then?" asked Malice.

"We searched the market up and down and found nuffink. Like I says: disappeared! Then Queenie stops turnin' up for work and her parlour boy Jack comes along with a message to say she's gone down with the ghost-chills and won't be around for a bit."

"Excuse me, did you say parlour boy?" said Malice.

"Yeah," said the baker. "'Is name's Jack, nice lad, very nimble."

Malice clapped her hands together in excitement.

"Jack is ace, he's very nimble!" she cried. "It's exactly like the riddle said!"

Uncle Vex slapped his thigh jovially.

"By Jupiter, you're right!" he said.

"And I would guess Jack is the same parlour

boy who bought all the stinging nettle tea from the Vengeful Brew!" Malice went on. "Grandads are very fond of stinging nettle tea."

"I would guess you're right again!" said Uncle Vex. "Well done! You really are good at riddles, aren't you?"

Malice grinned. But this was no time for revelling in smugness. They'd made progress but the case wasn't solved yet.

"Do you know where Queenie Florus lives?" Malice asked the baker.

"Dunno," said the baker. "But Frank might. Oi, Frank!" he shouted over towards a greengrocer's stall, where a man was shouting:

"Putrid veg! Everything a pand a pand. Worms and woodlice guaranteed!"

Frank looked over and grinned.

"'Allo Vex!" he shouted. "'Ow's it going?"

Malice and Uncle Vex thanked the baker for

his help and left him scratching his bottom as they crossed the alley to the greengrocer.

"Hello, Frank," said Uncle Vex. "How's business?"

"Booming, thanks to you," said Frank. "If you hadn't bamboozled those zombie tomatoes, I'd have had no customers left!"

"All part of the service," said Uncle Vex, taking a small bow.

"Are you the new apprentice?" Frank asked Malice cautiously. Before Malice could answer, he added: "Shame about that last one getting carried off by them trolls!"

Malice looked at her uncle again. Her uncle looked back and shifted uncomfortably under her stare.

"That was a most unfortunate turn of events," said Uncle Vex, wringing his hands. "It almost never happens!"

Malice turned back to Frank.

"Do you know where Queenie Florus lives?" she asked.

Frank sneezed and wiped his nose on a limp cabbage.

"'Fraid I can't 'elp you there," said Frank.

Malice's shoulders drooped along with her spirits. Every time she felt like she'd made a breakthrough, she came slap-bang up against another brick wall. "But she does like a glass of the old wasp-venom vino and a good knees-up down the King's Head Pub," Frank added ponderously. "Her and her grandad are regulars. If I was you, I'd head to the pub and ask there. Just keep going left, left, right, left, right, right, right, left, left and left, right, left, left and if you're lucky you'll be nearly there by then."

"Thank you, Frank," said Malice. "I think." She could feel her hopes rising again. At last they were getting closer to finding Grandad.

Malice and Uncle Vex set off in the direction

Frank had pointed in. Frank sneezed snottily on some spinach.

"I hope I'm not going down with the ghost-chills," he said.

LESS TALK, MORE RUNNING

The serpentine alleys of suburban Underland were lined with crooked buildings, bent over like old men with bad backs, so that their top windows almost touched. Lively ghosts bustled along in top hats and tails or crinoline dresses, sipping curdled cappuccinos. Newspaper sellers waved copies of the *Ghostly Times* and the *Daily Spook* hollering:

"Read all about it! Grandad-nappers At Large, Cosy Grandads Agency Suspects Ghoul-Play!"

A thick mist rolled in as Malice and Uncle Vex

trekked through the confusing maze of streets and snaked around their ankles in a smoky swirl. Every ghost they asked for directions to the King's Head Pub seemed to send them on a different path or suggest a short-cut that was anything but. Soon the mist was twisting up around their shoulders as they walked and turned, turned and walked. The damp air was making Malice's hair curl and Uncle Vex's quiff sag.

When the mist reached their heads, Uncle Vex pulled out a paper fan from his jacket pocket and wafted it in front of them, to clear the way and make sure they didn't stumble into lamp-posts.

They had just turned on to Guillotine Street, when a head without a body loomed out of the mists before them. Uncle Vex screamed and threw himself behind Malice. Malice, who had seen far worse things hidden in Pa's wardrobe, looked at the long-haired, moustachioed head without a body and asked:

"Is this the King's Head Pub?"

"Why yes, my dear, it is!" said the head. "And I am the King's Head of the aforementioned King's Head Pub. Delighted to make your acquaintance."

Malice gave a small curtsy and Uncle Vex bowed. The King's Head grinned a wide toothed grin and his moustache curled tighter.

"How may I be of assistance, my good lady?" asked the King's Head. "We serve a wide range of home-cooked meals – snake-and-kiddy pie, Skunk stew and plumplings!"

Malice didn't want to offend the King's Head but neither of those options sounded very appealing. Instead, she said:

"Golly, they sound delicious! But we've only just had lunch. We need to find Queenie Florus. Would you happen to know the way to her house?"

"Queenie Florus, you say!" said the King's Head. His head did a loop-the-loop in the air and then spun, sending his long hair flying outward into the mist.

"What a lady!" The King's Head exclaimed. "Such charm. Such flair!"

He stopped spinning and floated close to Malice's face, his expression suddenly pained.

"But tell me," he whispered urgently, "is she all right? I haven't seen her in days. I feel quite lonely without her. I've missed her sweet face, her tinkling laugh, the way she arm-wrestles werewolves and can down a pint of arsenic ale in under a minute…"

"Well, that's what we want to find out," said Malice. "Queenie and I have both lost our grandads. I'm hoping we can work together to find them."

"Lost your grandads, you say? Oh, you poor dear unfortunates. To lose one's grandad is almost as bad as losing one's body; I should know! And to think, all this time I was worried that she'd been charmed away by that dastardly Duke's Head on the Hangman's Road. What a fool I am!" he wailed and his eyes rolled around in their sockets. "How could I have doubted a

woman so foulsome-fair as Queenie Florus!"

The King's Head's caterwauling was causing the ghost-hounds to howl. Uncle Vex crouched in the gutter with his fingers in his ears.

"Do make him stop!" he pleaded.

Malice realized she would have to employ some minor mischief if she was ever going to get any information out of this melodramatic monarch.

"There is no need to fret, Your Highness." Malice interrupted the King's Head's groans. "If you tell us where Queenie lives, you could be instrumental in helping her find her lost grandad."

The King's Head stopped howling.

"I could?"

Malice nodded.

"And imagine how grateful Queenie would be to such an important member of the rescue team."

"You would be a hero!" added Uncle Vex.

The King's Head jutted his chin out regally.

"Indeed!" he boomed, his misery evaporating. "Oh, how I have loved her from afar. I'd like to ask her out on a date but I don't know if she'd be interested because, I'm, well, you know, just a head."

"But what a magnificent head you are!" Malice responded. "Yours is by far the best head I've seen in Underland!"

"Do you really think so?" asked the King's Head excitedly.

"Absolutely!" said Malice. "If you give us directions to Queenie's house, I'll be sure to put in a good word for you. Any lady would be honoured by the attentions of such a handsome head."

That settled it. The King's Head began to rattle off directions to Queenie's house– which were complicated and many – and Uncle Vex took out his investigator's notebook and pencil and scribbled them down.

They thanked the King's Head and waved him goodbye. The King's Head, having no body, winked and wiggled his moustache in return. As the mists swallowed the King's Head completely Malice smiled to herself as yet another piece of the witches' riddle slid into place: the King's Head was indeed a *Lonely King!* But maybe she could fix that.

It was easy to get lost in the streets of Underland, and Malice and her uncle became very good at it. One alley looked just like another, until you turned back the way you had come and found it looked nothing like it did a moment before.

They decided to stop for refreshments at a trendy coffee shop, run by a pair of vegan vampires called Lilith and Vlad. As eager as Malice was to find Queenie's house, it felt as though they had been walking for hours and she was sorely in need of some sustenance.

They sat outside the café, sipping their beetroot lattes at a black iron patio table with an empty

vase in the centre of the table, while the mists twisted around their mugs like vaporous vines.

"How far do you think it is to Queenie's house now?" asked Malice. The King's Head had told them that Queenie lived in Melancholy Square; "a very nice neighbourhood," he had said, "full of rapscallions, rogues and rascals."

Uncle Vex consulted his notebook.

"By my calculations," he said, "we are five-and three-quarter streets closer than we were twenty streets ago, but seven-and-three-fifths streets further away as the crow flies at midnight."

"That is completely nonsensical," said Malice.

"Thank you," said Uncle Vex.

At that moment a gangly boy skipped out of the café and jumped over a patio table with a candlestick at its centre. A basket laden with freshly cooked dead-fly biscuits swung wildly from his hand. Lilith and Vlad came out to wave him off.

"See you later, Jack!" called Vlad.

"Such a nice boy," said Lilith. "And so nimble!"

Malice jumped up from the table, upturning the dregs of their beetroot lattes and sending magenta liquid flying across the table.

"My suit!" cried Uncle Vex, blotting his trousers with a polka dot handkerchief.

"Jack, wait!" Malice called, waving her arms wildly.

"Sorry, no time!" shouted Jack over his shoulder. "I'm already late. They'll be wanting biscuits to go with their tea!"

"I'll never get these stains out," mumbled Uncle Vex.

"Come on!" shouted Malice, pulling her dismayed uncle up out of his chair. "That was Jack, the nimble parlour boy!"

"It was?" Uncle Vex exclaimed as Jack tore away with jackrabbit speed and disappeared into the mist.

"Oh me oh my! Follow that parlour boy!" shouted Uncle Vex.

Together they stumbled and tripped through the dense mist, narrowly avoiding lamp-posts and sniffing the air like bloodhounds, letting their noses lead them in the direction of the hot biscuits. The scent of freshly baked dead-fly biscuits was strong enough that Malice and Uncle Vex were able to follow the aroma through the milky fog, but no matter how fast they ran, they couldn't seem to catch up to the parlour boy. Jack's echoey footsteps were always way ahead of them.

"I hope you didn't ruin my suit for a wild ghost chase!" panted Uncle Vex.

"Never mind your suit," gasped Malice. "Less talk, more running!"

Eventually they rounded a corner and found

themselves sprinting alongside a set of railings – not unlike the ones in Felicity Square – which enclosed a patch of scrubby dead parkland with benches dotted about it. There was a sign attached to the railings which read: Melancholy Square.

"We made it!" Malice puffed. "If we can just follow the scent of biscuits to Queenie's house…"

But before she had time to finish her sentence, the slap of Jack's running feet came to an abrupt halt, a door slammed and the hot biscuit smell evaporated.

"Did you see which house he went into?" Uncle Vex panted hoarsely. He was bent double with his hands on his knees.

"No," said Malice. "Did you?"

The mist hung heavy in the square and only the occasional wrought iron gate or thorny bush punctured the dense whiteness.

Uncle Vex shook his head. "I was too busy trying to breathe and run," he said. "To *see* as well would

have been quite beyond me, I'm afraid."

"What now?" asked Malice, throwing her arms up in frustration. She was hot, she was tired, her beetroot latte had sloshed around so much in her stomach that she had a stitch in her side and she *still* hadn't found Grandad.

"I suppose we'll have to knock on every door until we find Queenie," said Uncle Vex. "Chin up now, old girl." He patted her awkwardly on the arm.

Suddenly, from above their heads there came a slurpy-sucking noise. Malice and Uncle Vex looked up and squinted into the dark sky. The tangle of sky-roots parted, scurrying backwards like retreating spiders to reveal a hole, and within the hole a vortex, swirling round and round like a tornado.

In another moment the hole puckered in on itself like a mouth chewing on a lemon and, with a loud burp, it spat a bemused, bespectacled grandad down a chimney at the furthest end of the street.

"There!" yelled Malice.

"Follow that chimney!" shouted Uncle Vex.

They arrived, huffing and puffing, outside the house to which the chimney belonged.

The townhouse was tall and twisted, with large sash windows and concave walls. They pushed at the gate and entered into a neat garden filled with headless stems swaying in the breeze, with steps leading up to the house. Malice was about to climb the steps to knock on the door but Uncle Vex caught her arm.

"Let's see what we're dealing with first," he said.

The front window was too tall for them to see into, so Malice scrambled up her uncle and stood on his shoulders – swaying like the stems in the garden – and peeked in.

The sitting room was cosy, with chintzy wallpaper and curtains, and a fire burning merrily in the hearth. And it was absolutely FULL of grandads!

There were grandads loafing on sofas, and playing pianos, and reclining on rugs. There were grandads in conference at coffee tables, arm-wrestling on armchairs, and bantering on benches. There were even grandads playing snooker and some were wheelbarrow racing. Some were doing both at the same time! This had to be the place, thought Malice. She could have leapt for joy, but she didn't think her uncle's shoulders could take the strain.

Each grandad had a floral cup and saucer, and a small plate of dead-fly biscuits by his side.

Malice scanned the room for *her* grandad but she couldn't see him.

"What can you see?" hissed Uncle Vex, holding tight to her ankles.

"Grandads," hissed Malice. "Grandads everywhere!"

"Let's get inside," said Uncle Vex.

NO GRANDAD GETS
LEFT BEHIND

Malice and Uncle Vex disentangled themselves and knocked loudly on the front door. It was opened, after some moments, by Jack.

"Hello, again!" said Jack. "Sorry I had to rush off. You know how grandads are about tea and biscuits!"

The sound of many kettles whistling and a chinking of china drifted up the hallway.

"Can we speak to Queenie Florus please?" asked Malice.

"Jack!" came a shrill voice. "Jack, where are you? The grandads need more tea!"

"They always do," said Jack, smiling and rolling his eyes. "Come on in. Welcome to grandad central!"

Jack led them down a long, crooked hall hung with framed paintings and Roman mosaics of smiling people wearing togas and laurel wreaths. They passed several rooms filled with comfortable grandads – Malice poked her head into each one, but none held her grandad – until they reached a large kitchen, with cups and saucers piled to the ceiling. Kettles puffed plumes of steam into the air.

A round-faced woman with red cheeks, and hair that had gone curly from the heat looked up as they entered. She was wearing a white toga with a floral pinny over the top and strappy sandals that she'd tied criss-cross halfway up her legs. Malice thought the

flowery pinny and toga made a strange outfit but she reasoned that most things in Underland were strange and she pushed the thought aside. "Queenie?" said Uncle Vex.

"Oh, Mr Vex investigator sir!" Queenie exclaimed. "You look just like your picture in the *Daily Spook*. Thank goodness you're here. I've been trying to get to your office but the grandads keep needing more and more tea, and I can't leave the poor things thirsty!"

"What's going on?" asked Malice. "Why are all these grandads here?"

"I never meant for this to happen!" said Queenie and her lip began to wobble. "I just wanted my grandad back!"

Queenie Florus burst into loud sobs and threw her arms around Malice's shoulders, wetting her pinafore through to the skin with her tears. Malice helped the weeping flower seller to a chair and Uncle Vex poured her a cup of tea.

"Now then," said Uncle Vex, stuffing several warm dead-fly biscuits into his pocket for later. "I think you'd better tell us everything."

Queenie took a slurp of tea and told her sorry tale. Once she'd started, she barely drew breath. There was no gap between either words or sentences for Malice to interject and ask where Grandad was. She was practically jigging on the spot with impatience, but she knew that if a puzzle was worth solving, it was worth solving properly. So, she steeled herself for what Grandad would call *the long game* and concentrated hard on Queenie's story.

Every day, Queenie and her grandad worked on the flower stall – they supplied all the tearooms of Underland with their stagnant stems. And every night, after supper, they played the piano and sang show tunes with Jack in the parlour.

One evening, just as they were finishing off a rousing rendition of *My Old Man's a Dustman*,

during which her grandad played the spoons, there was a sudden poof of smoke and Queenie's grandad was gone.

"Just like that!" Queenie wept, blowing her nose on her apron. "He disappeared!"

After two days of fruitless searching, she was desperate. She went down to the Be-Careful-What-You-Wish-For Emporium on the corner of Hex Street and bought a wish for two doubloons.

"Why didn't you come to me?" asked Uncle Vex. "I am an investigator, after all."

"I thought a wish would be quicker," Queenie replied. "And by the time I realized it wasn't, I had grandads dropping in all over the place. Grandads is a full-time job, you know!"

"Has your grandad ever gone missing before?" Malice asked gently.

"No," sniffed Queenie. "Not never, not once!"

"And he hadn't argued with any witches or

warlocks?" Uncle Vex asked, chewing his pencil thoughtfully. "Because we all know how irrational they are when angry. I wouldn't want to wrangle with a wrathful warlock!"

"Noooo!" Queenie broke into a wail at this and Malice pointed a frown at her uncle, who shrugged his shoulders innocently in return.

"There, there, Queenie," Malice soothed. Uncle Vex looked uncomfortable.

"I just want my grandad back!" sobbed Queenie. "So, I made a wish. I didn't know I'd get *all* the grandads! But they just keep dropping down my chimney. Not that I mind," Queenie went on. "I loves grandads! And I'm happy to have them here…" She gave a particularly large sob and a snot-bubble ballooned out of her left nostril. "But none of them are *MY* grandad!"

Malice knew just how she felt and was finally about to ask Queenie if *her own* missing grandad

had dropped down the chimney, when there came a

great shouting and crowing from the parlour.

"Wa-haa and woo-hoo! You lose, suckers!"

Malice and Uncle Vex looked at one another

"Grandad!" they chimed in unison.

They found Grandad in the parlour, sitting with several other grandads around a large green poker table. Malice's Grandad was scooping a pile of toffees towards himself, having just won a game.

"Grandad!" Malice exclaimed and threw her arms around him. She felt so relieved and happy to see his craggy old face, she thought she might laugh and cry at the same time. "Oh, Grandad, it's so good to see you. I've been terribly worried!"

"Hello, Malice, my love!" said Grandad. "I knew you'd find me; you're the cleverest Malign I know. I said to the boys," he motioned around the table to the wrinkly grandads, who were tens of decades past being boys, "my Malice's wits are needle sharp. She'll get to the bottom of this debacle."

The grandads around the table nodded their heads sagely in agreement.

Uncle Vex stepped forward.

"Hello," he said.

"Vexatious Malign! As I rot and crumble!" chuckled Grandad. "How are you, my boy?"

"Not too shabby, thanks," said Uncle Vex. "All the better for seeing you, that's for sure."

"Right," said Malice, tugging on Grandad's arm. "Let's get you home, Grandad."

"No can do, Ducky," said Grandad. "There's a spell on us grandads. No one can leave till it's broken!"

Malice felt her good mood evaporate. Surely she hadn't found her grandad only to have him stuck in Underland by a spell? She felt sure that if they set their minds to it, they could have Grandad back home in time for supper.

"What about if Uncle Vex and I keep a tight hold of you all the way back to Topside?" she asked.

Grandad looked at her sadly and shook his head.

"I don't think it'll work, Duck. Believe me, we've all tried to leave, but we wind up back here again. The spell won't let us go."

The other grandads and Jack nodded their heads in agreement. Queenie sighed. "I'm sorry," she said. "This is all my fault."

Malice shook her head stubbornly. She wouldn't believe it until she had tried it for herself – she was a great one for trying things for herself, was Malice.

"Right!" said Malice. "Uncle Vex, you take hold of one of Grandad's hands and I'll take the other. We're taking Grandad home. Hold on tight now!"

Malice and Uncle Vex took a hand each and led Grandad to the front door. A gaggle of grandads shuffled along the hall behind them to watch.

Queenie pulled open the front door. Grandad stood in the middle and Malice and Uncle Vex held his hands tightly on either side.

"One, two, three!" said Malice. And they stepped outside.

For a moment nothing happened. And then Grandad's hands became slippery like a bar of wet

soap. Malice and Uncle Vex tried to keep a hold of them, but his fingers slid from their grasp each time they tried to catch a hold of them. They threw their arms around Grandad, but he slurped out of their grip as if he were made of cooked spaghetti and, with a sound like a raspberry being blown through dribbly lips, he shot straight up into the air and plunged feet-first back down the chimney.

Everybody rushed into the sitting room in time to see the fireplace burp Grandad out on to the hearth rug, a little sooty but none the worse for his escapade.

Grandad looked up at Malice and shrugged.

"I'm sorry, Ducky," he said, seeing the disappointment on Malice's face. "I told you; none of us can leave until the spell is broken. And even if I could, there's more at stake here than just me." Grandad gestured to all the other grandads. "No grandad gets left behind," he said, taking Malice's hand in his. "You need to make it right for *all* of us."

Malice nodded.

"I understand, Grandad," she said.

Malice helped Grandad up and escorted him back to his place at the poker table. She desperately wanted her grandad home; she couldn't, wouldn't give up! Instead, she would channel her disappointment into determination and her sadness into a steely resolve.

Uncle Vex turned to Queenie, who stood in the doorway wringing her hands.

"Queenie," he said, "when you made your wish, what *exactly* did you wish for?"

"All I did was wish my grandad back," Queenie protested.

Malice remembered the shop-witches' words: "*The devil is in the detail.*"

"There must be more to it!" said Malice with certainty. "Think hard now, Queenie. What did you *actually* say?"

Queenie screwed her eyes up tight in concentration.

"I said, *I wish I may, I wish I might, have Grandad back within my sight!*" said Queenie.

"Nothing wrong with that," noted Uncle Vex.

"And then I said," Queenie went on. "*If I can't have a grandad, then no one can!*"

"Ah," said Uncle Vex, pursing his lips.

"I think that may be where the problem lies," agreed Malice.

"I didn't mean it!" said Queenie. "I was upset and it just popped out of my mouth."

"I'm afraid witches don't take into account things you might not mean," said Malice. "They take words very seriously. So, unless we find *your* grandad," she continued, piecing the puzzle together, "nobody else can have a grandad either."

Queenie looked down and smoothed her apron, her bottom lip pushed out into a sorrowful pout.

"I'd give anything to have my grandad back," said the woeful flower seller.

"I know," said Malice. She gave Queenie a hug. "Thank you for looking after my grandad for me in the meantime."

"Oh, you're very welcome, dear. He is delightfully cantankerous."

"I promise to do everything in my power to bring your grandad home to you," soothed Malice. "No grandad gets left behind." *Crikey!* she thought, *I'm breaking all the Malign family rules today with all this helpful do-gooding I'm undertaking.* Queenie gave each of Malice's cheeks a squeeze and a kiss.

"And I promise your grandad won't want for nuffink while you're gone," said Queenie.

Uncle Vex stuffed three dead-fly biscuits into his mouth.

"Well, we've solved the mystery of the disappeared grandads," he said, spitting dry biscuit crumbs on to the carpet as he spoke. "Now we need to find out why Queenie's grandad was disappeared in the first place

and break this bally spell once and for all!"

"How do we do that?" asked Malice.

"We investigate!" answered Uncle Vex.

14

THERE'S NOTHING WHATEVER THE MATTER WITH BEING UNUSUAL

Malice hugged Grandad tightly and promised him she would have him back home soon. She didn't want to leave him, but she felt all the better for knowing he was being well cared for.

"I'm all right, Duck," said Grandad. "There's as much stinging nettle tea as we can drink." Grandad winked at Jack, and Jack saluted in return. "And the chairs are comfy, and the dead-fly biccies are fresh."

Queenie took a portrait down from the wall. A friendly, fuzzy-white haired old man in a toga smiled out from the canvas. He was stood outside a Roman bathhouse, holding a basket of flowers. Curiously, Malice noted that the flowers still had their heads attached. She surmised the portrait must have been painted before he became a ghost; flowers with heads were apparently more of a Topsider thing.

"That's my grandad," said Queenie. "Just so's you know what he looks like."

Queenie and Jack waved Malice and Uncle Vex off. At the garden gate, Malice remembered her promise to the King's Head. She turned and called back:

"Queenie, you have an admirer. How do you feel about ghosts without bodies?"

Queenie blushed.

"Them's my favourite kinds of ghosts!" Queenie replied. "Specially that King's Head on Guillotine Street; his moustache makes me giddy as a ghoul-girl! He's got the best manners this side of the sewer."

Malice smiled with merry mischief. If things worked out the way she hoped, the King's Head would be a *lonely king* no more.

"Well, it just so happens that the King's Head has been *crucial* in helping us with the disappearing grandads case," said Malice.

Queenie clutched at her heart and smiled dreamily. "My hero!" she gushed .

The mist had begun to clear as Malice and Uncle Vex made their way back through the Underland maze to Uncle Vex's office.

When they reached the King's Head, he shouted: "Tally-ho, fair maiden! What news?" as they passed him.

"Well, we found my grandad," said Malice. "And a

hearty houseful of other grandads."

"And sweet Queenie's grandad?" asked the King's Head. "Is my love reunited with her relative?"

"Not yet," said Malice. "But we're working on it as we speak. By the way, you should definitely ask Queenie out on a date. She told me ghosts without bodies are her favourite kind and she likes your head best!" A wide smile broke across the King's face and his moustache curled in and out at the sides like a party-blower. Malice even thought she saw him blush.

"Ahh-whoop-dee-doooo!" shouted the King's Head, and he began to turn quadruple loop-the-loops in the air. Malice felt pleased to have made someone happy; she'd make a lot *more* people happy if she managed to find Grandad Florus!

They stopped in briefly at Vlad and Lilith's café and bought sandwiches to keep them going. As Lilith handed the paper packages over to Malice, she whispered in her Transylvanian accent:

"Do be careful, dear. Your uncle's last apprentice was carried away by giant eagles, never to be seen again."

Malice looked at her uncle.

"That was a most unfortunate turn of events," pouted Uncle Vex. "It almost never happens!"

Back at the office, Uncle Vex logged on to the Underweb. He typed "reasons for ghosts to go missing" into Gurgle, and they munched their pumpkin hummus sandwiches while they waited for the results.

The computer whirred as it searched and then with a MMWWAAHAHA it was ready.

REASONS FOR GHOSTS TO GO MISSING:

1. They need a holiday
2. They've been spellbound by a wicked sorcerer
3. Their grave has been disturbed

Malice and Uncle Vex studied the list. Numbers one and two seemed unlikely, given Queenie's insistence that Grandad Florus had never taken off before, and nor had he argued with anyone likely to spellbind him. But number three gave Malice an idea. Suddenly Queenie's outfit didn't seem so strange any more. In fact, if her idea was right, it made perfect sense.

"We need to find Seth," said Malice.

"How on earth is a paperboy going to help us find a missing ghost?" asked Uncle Vex.

"Seth told me there was a Roman graveyard discovered on the site of the new shopping centre," Malice replied.

"And?" said Uncle Vex.

Malice jabbed her finger at the computer screen.

"*Their grave has been disturbed!*" she said. "What if Grandad Florus's remains were buried in the graveyard and they've been dug up? That could be why he disappeared."

"My dear niece, Grandad Florus's bones could be buried anywhere!"

"You saw what Queenie was wearing, didn't you?" Malice asked.

"A very fetching toga ensemble," replied Uncle Vex. "Though I'm not sure the pinny was the right choice to go with it…"

"Never mind the pinny!" Malice said, exasperated. "In what period of history did people wear togas?"

Uncle Vex waved his hand in the air nonchalantly.

"Well, there were the ancient Greeks and the Romans…" He stopped short. "Ah, yes. I see your point."

"Grandad Florus is Roman. A Roman graveyard has just been discovered. It is too great a coincidence for them not to be connected. And Seth knows where the Roman graveyard is. He's my friend, he'll want to help."

Uncle Vex ran his fingers through his enormous quiff, then he jumped to his feet and shouted:

"Let's go!"

Uncle Vex ushered Malice into the large leather trunk next to the filing cabinet and climbed in behind her. He pulled the lid closed over their heads and lit a flaming torch on the wall. As he did so, there was a sputtering sound, and torches all around them flickered into life, revealing a long flight of stairs spiralling up and away into the distance.

The walls were cold grey stone, and a handrail made of thick rope, worn smooth and waxy by time, was held to the walls by black iron rings. The air was chilly and Malice shivered. Somewhere, a drip of water *plink-plinked* unseen, and the sound of it echoed around the staircase. This was another secret gateway between Underland and Topside. Malice wondered how many there were, dotted all over and under the place.

They climbed up and around and up and around. The stone steps were dipped in the middle from many pairs of feet making the same laborious climb over the centuries. As they climbed, Uncle Vex told her old stories of Topunders using gateways like this to escape pitchfork-waving Topsiders or to hide their smuggled loot from the Topside authorities. Uncle Vex knew a lot about Topunder history. His tales of wild chases and spectacular treasure hoards took Malice's mind off their climb through the earth and the burning in her leg muscles.

Eventually they reached the top, a smooth mud roof with skinny plant roots dangling down from it. There was a trapdoor lying flat in the earthy ceiling above their heads. Uncle Vex inserted a key, turned it, and pushed upwards. The trapdoor flipped open with a creak.

Malice found herself looking up at stars glinting through gaps in leafy branches. Uncle Vex poked

his head out to check the coast was clear and they scrambled out of the roots at the base of the old oak tree in Felicity Square.

It was dark now. The houses in the square had their curtains drawn, and a warm orange glow shone through the gaps. Malice imagined tea and hot crumpets and soft furry cushions within. Malice turned and looked at her own home. Malignant House loomed, cold and foreboding, its turrets piercing the clouds above, the crooked windows grey and lifeless. Malice sighed. Uncle Vex must have guessed how she was feeling because he tugged softly at her sleeve and said kindly:

"You know the grass isn't always greener. It may look lush from afar, but when you get up close it might be full of weeds and cowpats. Come on, old girl, lead the way." And they set off towards Affable Street where Seth lived.

As they walked, Malice noticed the streets seemed

darker than usual. She looked up and saw that all the bulbs had been stolen from the street lamps.

"Is that Pa's handiwork?" asked Uncle Vex.

"It looks like it," said Malice wearily. "Malign mischief-making at its most menacing."

They turned into Affable Street where the houses were squished together as if huddling to keep warm, and stopped outside a house with a green door, which had a round window with stained-glass patterns cut into the top. The warm light from within spilled out on to a little winding path, lined with wildflowers.

Malice gently plucked a passing moth out of the air and whispered something to it. The moth flew away and came back moments later with fifty of its friends. Then they fluttered up to the smallest window at the top of the house and began to beat their wings against the glass.

"You've been practising!" Uncle Vex commented. He looked impressed.

"Of course!" said Malice. Grandad had told Malice how Ma used to have all sorts of magic she'd inherited from Nana, but because she hadn't bothered to practise, it had all but disappeared. Now the only spells Ma had left were for making stink-bombs and blowing up cabbages. Malice was determined not to make the same mistake.

Presently the window opened and Seth poked his head out.

"Hallo, Malice!" he whispered loudly. "Nice moth-whispering. Any news on Grandad?"

"Plenty," Malice whispered back. "But now we need your help!"

"Like I said – anytime!" Seth grinned. "Are we going on an adventure?"

"Yes!" Malice called. "Bring your bike."

A moment later Seth slipped out of the house and retrieved his bike from behind the rhododendron bush. He was wearing his favourite puffer body-

warmer over a checked shirt and his trusty satchel across his body. Seth's jeans were always holey at the knees despite his dad constantly patching them; overall, Seth had the rumpled look of a person who liked to climb trees, crawl through undergrowth and get caught up in capers.

The front door opened again and Seth's dad stood in the doorway. Uncle Vex dived for cover behind a hydrangea out of force of habit; private investigators are used to creeping unseen amongst the shadows, it helps to keep a low-profile when solving mysteries.

"Hello, Malice," said Seth's dad, Bill. "I hear you're going on an adventure!"

"Yes," said Malice. "Some disappeared grandads need reappearing." She pointed to the bush, which was quivering. "That's my Uncle Vex. He's an investigator."

"Not Vexatious Malign?" said Bill, squinting into the undergrowth.

Uncle Vex stepped gingerly out from behind the hedge.

"I was just, er, checking for blackfly. You can't be too careful when it comes to garden pests."

"It *is* you!" said Seth's dad.

Uncle Vex stopped pretending to examine the bush then and looked up.

"Bill Pinkerton!" Uncle Vex exclaimed. "I don't believe it!"

The two men shook hands warmly.

"We were best friends at school!" said Bill. "How many years has it been?"

"At least twenty-five," answered Uncle Vex. "You haven't changed a bit."

"Neither have you!" said Bill. "You're still wearing your hair in that quiff, I see."

Uncle Vex chuckled and preened his hair.

"Come round for tea one night and we'll have a catch up," added Bill.

"Don't mind if I do!" agreed Uncle Vex. "Bill Pinkerton; well shiver my timbers and call me a shipwreck, it's good to see you."

"You too, old friend."

Seth's other dad Pete joined Bill at the door, and they waved the three adventurers off into the night.

As Malice, Seth and Uncle Vex set off down the dark streets, Malice said:

"I thought Maligns didn't usually have friends?"

"I'm not a usual Malign," said Uncle Vex. He winked at Malice. "And there's nothing whatever the matter with being unusual!"

"So, you're saying it's OK to have friends," said Malice.

"Let me put it this way," said Uncle Vex thoughtfully. "I'd rather be the oddest oddball in the oddball ball-pit any day of the week and have interesting friends, than be a bog-standard Boris in a box of banality with all the other bog-standards!"

Malice smiled. "I'll take that as a yes," she said.

Uncle Vex nodded.

"Now that we've cleared that up," said Seth, "what are we doing on this adventure?"

"Visiting an ancient graveyard, discovering whether a grave has been disturbed and, if so, restoring the missing bones to a place of rest in order to reappear a disappeared grandad," said Malice.

"Brilliant!" exclaimed Seth.

NOT YOUR
AVERAGE SUNDAY

Uncle Vex secured the rope around his waist, checked the laces on his roller-skates and gave the *OK* signal. Malice perched on the back of the saddle with her arms around Seth's waist. Seth began to peddle, and Uncle Vex was pulled along behind.

Seth rode extraordinarily fast along the cycle lanes and through parks. As he did, Malice filled him in on their investigations so far and her hunch about Grandad Florus's bones being unburied at the

shopping centre site.

"Not your average Sunday," shouted Seth.

"Not even slightly!" Malice hollered back.

Malice always enjoyed a high-speed cycle with Seth but when she looked back at Uncle Vex, he was swaying wildly like a windswept water-skier.

Even in the dim twilight she could see his cheeks were bilious green.

The site for the new shopping centre was vast and floodlit, and cordoned off by a high wire fence. Inside, at one end, a security guard snoozed in his

Portakabin, a large guard dog sleeping peacefully at his feet. At the other end of the site, a group of people in high-vis jackets were digging, while another group were heaving large stones and carrying bags of archaeological finds out of an excavation tent and putting them carefully into the back of a van, which had *Yesteryear Museum* written on its side.

"That's the graveyard site," whispered Seth, pointing to where the work was happening.

They dismounted, then they walked – Uncle Vex tottering slightly in his skates – as quietly as they could around the edge of the fence and ducked down behind a yellow digger.

"We need to sneak in and see if Grandad Florus's bones are in that van with the rest of the artefacts," said Malice.

"Are you sure?" asked Uncle Vex, with a tinge of fear in his voice.

"It's the only way," replied Seth.

"Maybe I should hide here," said Uncle Vex. "I mean, *wait* here! Maybe I should *wait* here, as a lookout."

Malice and Seth raised their eyebrows. Seth parked his bike and the two friends crept around the perimeter fence. About halfway along they found a gap and slipped through it and on to the building site. The work crew were too busy carefully dusting bits of old pottery to notice them as they sidled alongside the van and looked in.

Inside, the van was full of bones in clear plastic bags, boxes of Roman coins and curios, and muddy clay urns. Malice leaned close to Seth's ear and whispered, "I'm going to climb in and look for Grandad Florus's bones. You cause a distraction so they don't see me."

Seth nodded.

"Be careful!" he hissed.

Then he ran noiselessly back over to the gap in the fence, ducked back through to the other side, and shouted:

"Hey there! I think my dog has fallen into one of your holes; he slipped through a gap in the fence. I can hear him but I can't see him. Can you help me?"

The baggers and diggers stopped what they were doing and walked over to Seth. Malice saw her chance. She climbed into the back of the van and quickly began to check the bags for signs of Grandad Florus's remains. Luckily the boxes and bags were all labelled with contents descriptions, allowing Malice to quickly discount them from her search. Then there were the urns: clay pots that held the remains of Roman bones which had been cremated. These were

carefully wrapped in sheets and sackcloth ready for transportation. *Phew*, thought Malice. *There's a lot to go through!*

Outside, Seth and the work crew were searching for his imaginary dog and Uncle Vex cowered – or rather, waited – behind the yellow digger.

Malice was still working her way through the artefacts, gently unwrapping the sheets on the painted urns and checking for clues that might pertain to Grandad Florus, when the foreman blew his whistle.

"Come on, you lot," he shouted. "That's enough. We've got to get these artefacts over to the museum for analysis. The lad will have to look for his dog on his own."

Then everything began to happen at once.

The crew reluctantly left Seth and started back towards their workstations and the van.

In the meantime, Uncle Vex had wobbled his way around the perimeter in his roller-skates and

crawled through the gap in the fence in order to offer assistance to Seth and Malice. Unfortunately, the wind was blowing the wrong way and funnelled Uncle Vex's lavender scent straight up the guard dog's nostrils, causing him to wake up in a foul mood and make chase, immediately bounding, barking and slobbering towards Uncle Vex with a maniacal glint in his bloodshot eyes; that dog hated the smell of lavender.

Trying to cause another distraction to give Malice time to get out of the van, Seth ran after the workers waving his arms, but only succeeded in tripping over a bronze centurion's head and falling headlong into a grave. His cries for help were lost beneath the sounds of an angry dog creating merry hell somewhere across the site.

Malice was about to jump down from the van,

when the sackcloth from one of the urns towards the back, slipped down to reveal a shock of white painted hair. In a flash she scrambled over to it and rubbed the mud from the clay pot with her sleeve. The same friendly face as in the portrait at Queenie's house smiled out at her.

"Found you!" said Malice, and she hugged the urn to herself triumphantly.

There came the crunch of heavy boots and raised voices outside and Malice realized that she'd run out of time to escape.

She looked around wildly for somewhere to hide. Her gaze fell upon a wooden packing crate and with no time to spare she folded herself, along with Grandad Florus's urn, into it and pulled down the lid, which locked itself shut with a CLICK.

The foreman slammed the van doors shut and banged the side with his fist.

"On your way!" he shouted.

The engine started with a roar and the van bumped and skidded on the uneven ground and left the building site with Malice locked inside it. The foreman yelled: "All right, you motley crew, tea-break, half an hour!"

The workers downed tools and sloped off to the twenty-four-hour cafe round the corner.

In their haste for builder's tea and rock cakes, they didn't notice the snazzily dressed man, skating for

his life over and around mounds of earth with the slathering guard dog hot on his heels. The guard, whose dog was terrorizing Uncle Vex, remained fast asleep, thanks to an app his wife had downloaded to his phone of soothing whale sounds.

Seth tried to scrabble out of the grave but it was too deep and all his efforts only made him look more rumpled than usual. He wouldn't have minded but the bones had already been removed. *And what*, thought Seth, *was the point of being stuck in an ancient grave if there were no ancient bones in it?*

Across the site, the guard dog had drawn close enough to nip at the back of Uncle Vex's jacket. Uncle Vex yelped as he skated. Just as it looked as though Uncle Vex was about become a dog's dinner, a big black bird swooped out the of the darkness and screeched:

"*Dead-fly biccies, dead-fly biccies, dead-fly biccies!*"

Uncle Vex remembered the biscuits he had taken from Queenie's house. He dug into his pocket, pulled out the biscuits and flung them over his shoulder. The dog – who was partial to a biscuit – instantly stopped the chase and settled down to snaffle the dead-fly treats.

With the dog occupied, Uncle Vex rushed to help Seth. He threw the end of the rope which was still tied around his waist down into the grave that had swallowed Seth. Seth grabbed hold of the end and Uncle Vex gripped a bulldozer to secure himself as Seth used the rope to heave himself out.

"Thanks, Malice's uncle," Seth panted, as he brushed the mud off his knees.

"Call me Vex," said Uncle Vex.

"Righty-ho. We have to get to the Yesteryear Museum,"

"Agreed," said Uncle Vex. "Follow that niece!"

Malice's journey to the museum had been surprisingly comfortable. The crate she was locked inside was filled with shredded paper, to keep precious artefacts safe in transit, and had acted as a rather comfortable mattress during the ride. She'd tried pushing against the lid of her crate, but it was sealed fast. The driver was singing power-ballads at the top of his voice and Malice was glad of the paper insulation around her ears.

When the van had arrived at the museum, everything was unloaded, including Malice. The workers grumbled as they carried Malice in her crate down the long corridors.

"This one's heavy!" said the first man.

"I wonder what's in it?" said the other.

"Probably old rocks," the first man responded. "These history types love their old rocks."

"Could be treasure," the other man suggested.

"Roman treasure. I'd like to see that."

Malice heard his companion suck air in through his teeth as he pondered this idea. "All right. Let's open it when we get to the storage room and find out," he said.

Oh no! thought Malice. *Now I'm really in trouble!*

If only she knew how to make herself invisible like Uncle Vex. But she hadn't learned how to do that yet. *Think think think!*

Malice could make out rows of display cases through a hole in the crate, as it was carried, rather roughly, through the museum. She heard a set of double doors swoosh open and then the crate was lowered to the ground.

"Right," said the first man. "Let's get it open and see what's inside."

From inside the crate, Malice could hear the squeaking and scratching of tools prying at the wooden lid and knocking against the lock.

Malice thought quickly. She would have to make

use of the skills she did have instead of worrying about the ones she didn't. She knew a lot about ghosts. And she knew all about their techniques for haunting Topsiders. Of course she did – her parents ran a haunting agency! Ma and Pa had taught her few tricks of the trade, like making your voice sound far away and then bouncing it around the room so that it seems to come from all angles. Malice covered her mouth with her hands and began to make ghostly moaning noises.

"AAAAAAWWWWWOOOOOOOOOOOOO!"

The men stopped trying to open the crate.

"W-what was that?" said the first man.

The other man cocked his head to listen and then said: "It's nothing. Keep going."

Malice began to moan again, louder this time.

"AAAAWWWAAOOOOOO!" she howled. "SET MEEEEE FREEEEE

AAAAAWWAAAAOOOOOOOO!
RELEASE THE CURSE OF THE
MUMMY'S TOMB!"

"Right," squeaked the first man. "That's it. I'm
outta here!"

"Wait for me!" squealed the other.

Malice heard the doors swish closed and the men's
voices and footsteps grow fainter as they hurried
away down the corridor. She sighed with relief.

"Phew, that was close, eh, Grandad Florus?" she
said to the urn she was still clutching to her chest.

When she was sure she was alone, Malice began
to push and shove at the lid. It still wouldn't budge.
She was sure that Seth and Uncle Vex would be on
their way to the museum, but how would they know
where to find her? The last place they would think
to look was inside an old packing crate. Malice
pondered this problem hard. And then the solution
came to her.

She pursed her lips and made a tiny whispering sound like the noise made by a moth rubbing its wings together. After a few moments a small brown moth fluttered in through the hole in the crate and settled on Malice's outstretched finger.

"Find Seth for me, pretty one," said Malice in moth-speak. "And lead him to me. Please hurry."

The moth beat its wings together, showering Malice in its glittery dust, before fluttering back out through the hole and disappearing into the dark museum.

***

Seth and Uncle Vex stood looking up at the solid wooden doors to the Yesteryear Museum. The street was empty and quiet.

"How do we get in?" asked Seth.

Uncle Vex was about to speak, when a shimmering

cloud appeared from the side of the building and headed straight for them. Uncle Vex dived behind Seth, but Seth only laughed as the delicate swarm of moths fluttered about his head.

"They want us to follow them," said Seth.

"I knew that," said Uncle Vex, straightening up.

The moth cloud flitted back around the side of the building and hovered up by a small open window on the second floor.

"I can't fit through that!" said Uncle Vex.

"No," said Seth. "But I can. You wait by the front door and I'll let you in."

And with that, Seth shimmied up the drainpipe and clambered in through the window, the moths flittering after him.

Uncle Vex hid in the shadows until, a few minutes later, Seth heaved the big wooden door open just enough for him to squeeze in through.

"It's well creepy here at night!" said Seth delightedly.

The dim light of the entrance hall seemed to flicker as the moths hovered in a low cloud waiting for the two adventurers to follow their lead. The moths led them down corridors, hung with beady-eyed portraits of lords and ladies. Past glass cabinets full of stuffed stoats and taxidermy tarantulas. Finally, they reached a door with a sign which read: "Roman Artefacts".

Seth pushed the door and it opened to reveal a long hall, split into aisles like a supermarket. The moths flew over to a packing crate and settled on it, like a tablecloth of velvet.

"Malice?" whispered Seth, hurrying over.

Malice heard his voice and began to bang on the lid.

"Help!" came her muffled voice. "I'm locked in."

Uncle Vex sprang into action with his trusty lockpick – Maligns were excellent lock-pickers – and in no time at all the lid sprang open and Malice was free. The moths, having completed their mission, rose

up in a flutter of gossamer wings and flittered off to find some tasty drapes to nibble.

"Nice moth-whispering!" said Seth.

"Thanks," said Malice gratefully. "Nice lock-picking, Uncle Vex."

"Thanks," said Uncle Vex, blushing. "Nice climbing," he said to Seth.

The three friends grinned at each other and then their eyes fell upon the vast hall and its many aisles with ancient artefacts lining the shelves. Box upon trunk upon crate of historical finds: pottery, vases, plates, tools and bronze statues turned green over the centuries, were stacked almost to the ceiling

"How are we ever going to find Grandad Florus's bones?" asked Seth. "There are thousands of boxes to go through!"

"No need." Malice grinned. "I've got them right here."

She held up the urn she had hidden along with

209

herself in the crate.

"You're amazing!" said Seth.

"Thank you," replied Malice.

"Good work, everyone," said Uncle Vex. "Now, let's get out of here. Seth, is there any chance you could cycle slightly slower on the way back?"

Seth laughed and promised he would try. But Seth's idea of slightly slower and Uncle Vex's were rather different. And when they arrived back at Felicity Square, Uncle Vex's face was greener than ever.

They sat on a bench in the residents' garden and considered what their next move should be.

"This is all well and good," said Seth, resting his hand on the urn. "But how does it help us reunite Grandad Florus with Queenie?"

"Well," said Uncle Vex, stroking his chin. "If we assume Grandad Florus disappeared because his urn was unburied…"

"Then we should be able to reappear him by

reburying his urn!" said Malice.

"Precisely," agreed Uncle Vex.

"But where?" wondered Seth. "It has to be somewhere safe. We can't put him back in the burial site. And you can't go around burying Roman artefacts in people's back gardens!"

Malice jumped up.

"Seth, you're a genius!" she exclaimed.

"I am?" queried Seth.

"Where is Melancholy Square in relation to Felicity Square?" Malice asked Uncle Vex.

"Why, it's directly below it," Uncle Vex answered.

"Perfect!" exclaimed Malice.

"Is that important?" asked Seth.

"I think it could be helpful," said Malice thoughtfully. "I think if we were to lay Grandad Florus's remains to rest somewhere very close to his Underland home, he might have a better chance of

finding his way back to Queenie."

"It's a sound idea," Uncle Vex mused. "But we still have the problem of where exactly to lay them. You are unpopular enough in Felicity Square, without digging up the residents' garden as well!"

A smile spread across Malice's face. "What do we have in the gardens of Malignant House?" she asked.

"Wild boar, pixies, quicksand…" listed Uncle Vex.

"Yes," said Malice. "But what else?"

Uncle Vex and Seth shrugged.

"The Malign family mausoleum!" said Malice.

"The what?" Seth blurted out.

"The mausoleum," said Malice. "It's like a stone house where our ancestors are buried."

"You have dead people buried in your garden?" asked Seth.

"Yes," said Malice calmly. "Hundreds."

"Cool!" said Seth.

WEIRDNESS MAKES THE WORLD GO ROUND

Malice did a quick check around the house to make sure her parents weren't home yet from mischief-making. Then she leaned out of one of the turret windows with her telescope and surveyed the grounds to make sure they weren't enjoying a moonlit bog-bath with fox-poo-facemasks, which is how they liked to wind down after a hard night's mischief. It really wouldn't do for Ma and Pa to find Uncle Vex and Seth on Malign property; Malice

would be grounded for a million years!

When she was sure the coast was clear, Malice heaved open the creaking iron gates to the gardens and Uncle Vex and Seth sneaked in. They hiked through towering grasses and clambered across bogland so muddy their feet got suctioned into its cold, damp depths. Malice was still holding Grandad Florus's urn tightly. Uncle Vex very nearly lost a shoe and Malice and Seth had to heave at his spindly legs until the bog gave him up with a disgruntled farty-slurp.

"Ah, the old playground," said Uncle Vex wistfully, shaking bog sludge out of his shoe. "Me dismantling bear traps while your pa snuffled for slugs. We spent many a happy hour out here dodging Great Grandad Malign's flaming arrows. Halcyon days!"

Finally, they reached a clearing in which there stood a pale marble building, rather like a Roman temple, with columns at its entrance and bats resting on the roof. Stone gargoyles stared out from the walls

of the mausoleum like goggle-eyed sentries and mythical marble creatures prowled the friezes with teeth bared to ward off strangers. Uncle Vex mopped his brow and steadied himself against a large gravestone in the pet cemetery that surrounded the mausoleum. The inscription on the gravestone read: "Here Lies Hex, Beloved Hellhound."

"Who was Hex?" asked Seth.

"Our dog," Malice replied. "Pa used to saddle him up and I'd ride on his back. He was the biggest hellhound in Britain." Malice smiled fondly at the memory.

"And the oldest. He could eat a side of beef in two bites," said Uncle Vex, dabbing away a tear with his handkerchief. "He was a great comfort to me growing up in Malignant House. His mournful baying never failed to help me drift off into a peaceful slumber."

Seth raised an eyebrow and said earnestly, "I really enjoy your family's weirdness."

"Thank you," Malice replied.

Malice heaved at the doors to the mausoleum and they begrudgingly groaned open into the musty building. Seth surveyed the scene with wonder as they walked between stone tombs and dusty sarcophagi. Holes had been hollowed out of the chalky white walls to house urns and grinning skulls. There was an archway at the far end of the room with a staircase.

"That goes down to the catacombs," explained Malice.

"Please can we find Grandad Florus a nice spot?" Seth begged. "Please! I've always wanted to see an underground burial chamber."

Malice laughed. "All right then," she said. "But don't wander off." It was a bit like the minotaur's maze down there, though Malice was reasonably sure there wasn't actually a minotaur roaming the stone halls.

The three friends made their way down to the catacombs and looked for a suitable place to lay

Grandad Florus's urn. Malice found a cosy spot, beside the tombs of Lord Odious Malign the Fourth and Lady Insidious Malign the Unrepentant, and laid Grandad Florus's urn between them.

"Should we say a few words?" asked Seth.

"If you like," said Malice.

They all three laid their hands on the old Roman pot.

"Dear Grandad Florus," said Seth. "We hope you find Queenie again."

"Here, here!" chimed Uncle Vex.

"Here, here!" echoed Malice.

As they made their way back through the gardens, the dawn light was turning the black sky to grey. Ma and Pa still weren't back from making mischief; they must have had a very busy night. So, Malice invited Uncle Vex and Seth in for a cup of cocoa.

Seth was beyond excited to see inside Malice's house but Uncle Vex was twitchy with nerves that Ma and Pa would come home unexpectedly and

find him. Things had never been right between the brothers ever since Uncle Vex had refused to take his G.O.O.N.S (General Odious Occupational Nuisance Skills) and join the family business, choosing instead to study sociology and criminology at university. By the time he had founded the detective agency, relations between them had turned from sour grapes to putrefied durian fruit.

"What now?" asked Seth, when they were settled in the cavernous kitchen with the fire burning in the hearth.

"Now we wait," said Malice. "If Queenie gets her grandad back, it should break the spell and all the other grandads should be able to return home."

Malice spoke with confidence but her stomach was a flutter with nervous butterflies. Had they done enough to counter Queenie's unwitting wish? Would the grandads be able to find their way home? She had her fingers crossed, her toes crossed inside her

boots and a four-leaf clover in her pocket for luck. The clover was a gift from a pixie whose wing she had fixed after he'd had an altercation with a fractious magpie last summer.

They sat around the battered old table, still littered with yesterday's swag, hugging their hot mugs and waiting. After the excitement of the night before, they were subdued now. The kitchen ghosts floated about here and there, quite oblivious to Malice and her companions, acting out the same chores they had performed centuries earlier: kneading phantom dough for bread and pushing ghostly sheets through the mangle. Seth couldn't see the kitchen ghosts – only Grandad had given his permission to be seen – so Malice gave him a running commentary of the bustling apparitions.

The sun was almost fully up. Malice and Seth were warming their feet by the fire, and Uncle Vex's eyes were slowly drooping to a close, when there

came a rumbling from beneath their feet, then a shuddering that seemed the shake the walls, and then a PPSSSSSHHHHH WWHHHOOOPPP! And Grandad popped up through the kitchen floor. He looked surprisingly unscathed by his adventure. On the contrary, he was wearing a newly knitted scarf decorated with stag-beetle pom-poms, and his cheeks had plumped out, probably as a result of all those dead-fly biscuits.

"Grandad!" shouted Malice. "I'm so happy to see you!" A mixture of relief and joy surged through her, from her toes to the top of her head.

"I'm happy to see you too, Ducky!" said Grandad, shaking his limbs out. "I'm happy to see all of you." He saw Seth and gave him a wink. "I could have guessed you'd be part of the team, young man."

"Glad you're back, Grandad," answered Seth, grinning proudly.

"Well done, all of you! You broke the spell and set us all free. Ooh, it's good to be back!"

"We couldn't have done it without Malice," said Uncle Vex.

"I don't doubt it!" agreed Grandad. "She's got a big heart and sharp wits, has my granddaughter."

Grandad threw himself down into an armchair by the fire and pulled a snow globe from his waistcoat. He passed it to Malice.

"Queenie asked me to give you this," he said.

Uncle Vex and Seth drew closer as Malice shook the snow globe. As the snowflakes settled, a scene, like an old black-and-white movie, began to play. It was Queenie and Grandad Florus and the King's Head. They were dancing in Queenie's parlour and Jack was playing the old piano. When the music stopped, they all turned and blew raspberries out towards Malice, Seth and Uncle Vex; a good, long raspberry is the traditional way for Underlanders to show their affection.

"Queenie got her grandad back!" Malice smiled. "And the King's Head found his Queenie."

"And I got to come home to my family," said Grandad happily. He looked at the three unlikely friends from his armchair and nodded.

"You three did good," he said. "I mean it. Really, really good!"

The front door opened and a roaring filled the house:

"WHO IS USING THE 'G' WORD IN MY HOUSE? WE DO NOT HELP AND WE DO NOT DO G-G-G-GOOD!"

Malice's parents were back.

"Hide!" hissed Malice.

Seth climbed into a cupboard with a skeleton named Critchly.

"Whoa!" he whispered. "A real live skeleton!" The skeleton waved and then held out a bony hand for Seth to shake, as it pulled the door closed on them with the other. As Seth's face disappeared into the darkness, Malice thought she had never seen him look happier.

Uncle Vex grabbed a frilly lampshade from the top of a pile of swag and stood in the corner with it on his head, his long, skinny legs easily passing for a lampstand. The tassels which ran around the bottom of the shade trembled as Uncle Vex quivered inside it.

"Calm yourself, boy," soothed Grandad, and handed Uncle Vex a toffee beneath his lampshade.

Meanwhile, Malice hastily piled the extra mugs into the sink, where a kindly ghost rinsed them clean and put them away. Just in time, she scooted back over to Grandad and the two of them stood side by side, awkwardly trying to look casual. Malice looked towards the cupboard where Seth was hiding and hoped the smell of the bog-mud on his jeans would mask the smell of his Topsiderness. Then she plastered a smile on her face as Ma and Pa burst into the kitchen. Antipathy-Rose toddled along behind, chewing on a plank of wood.

"Grandad!" exclaimed Pa. "You're back!" The jolly smile on Pa's face was quite unnerving, his gums pulled back over his brown teeth like a chimpanzee grinning.

"Thanks to Malice," said Grandad. "She outwitted some pretty wily witchy wishes!"

"We were so worried!" said Ma, softly for a change.

"You were?" Malice and Grandad said together.

"Course we were!" said Ma.

"The Haunting Agency really didn't have anything to do with the missing grandads!" Malice said happily. It was refreshing to be proved wrong about her parents' wrongdoing.

"What a ridiculous idea!" blustered Pa. He genuinely looked as though such an idea was repugnant to him.

"Your grandad is a right pain in the bum," said Ma. "But he's *our* pain in the bum and we wouldn't have it any other way!"

Ma smiled. Not a smirk or a sneer. An actual smile.

Pa sniffed the air.

"What's that stink?" he asked sternly.

Ma joined Pa.

"Smells like lavender soap and hair gel," said Ma. "The stink of Vexatious Malign!"

Malice looked sideways over to where her uncle was doing a good impression of a standard lamp. The tassels on the lampshade shook furiously. Looking around for something to distract them, Malice noticed her parents were clutching stacks of paper in their dirty hands.

"What are you holding?" Malice asked her parents.

"Nothing!" replied Ma and Pa together, thrusting their hands behind their backs and edging towards the kitchen door. But Malice had caught sight of the writing on the paper. "Have You Seen This Grandad?"

She felt a fuzzy warm feeling in her chest. *So that was why they were so late home,* thought Malice. They were out searching for Grandad and handing out fliers. Her parents would never admit to it and there was no point Malice trying to make them; it was

enough for her to know that they cared.

Just as the door was almost closed, Pa popped his head back round it. "Err. Ahem. Thanks, Malice," he whispered. "You did g-g-g-g…" The word stuck in his throat. He looked like a cat being sick. "Well done," he said finally. "I'm right proud of you!"

Malice smiled. Pa gave her a wink. "Don't tell your ma," he smiled back, and closed the door.

Malice listened to the yawns and farts and the shuffling sound of feet on the stairs as her parents made their weary way to bed. When she was sure they were at least three flights up, Malice gave a knock on the cupboard door and ruffled the tassels on Uncle Vex's lampshade to let them know the coast was clear.

Seth and Uncle Vex came gingerly out of hiding. Seth had been showing Critchly his Gruesome Ghoul card collection. He'd let Critchly have a couple of his doubles to get him started and the skeleton rattled his jawbone in delight.

"Well, I never thought I'd see the day!" offered Uncle Vex, bending his quiff back into shape. "Old Ma and Pa gone all sentimental, who'd have thought it?"

"There's nowt so queer as folk," mused Grandad.

"And thank goodness for that," Seth declared. "They say weirdness makes the world go round."

"I don't think they do," pondered Uncle Vex.

"Well then they should," said Malice. "And do you know what else? I think we make a g-g-g-g...pretty great team."

"Yes," mused Uncle Vex. "I've been thinking about that! I could do with some extra investigative help. What do you say, you two? Fancy a spot of amateur Underland sleuthing?"

"Count me in!" volunteered Seth. "Me and my trusty bike are at your service!"

"Good," said Uncle Vex. "And what about you, Malice? You could be my new apprentice. It would appear that my previous apprentices became ...

unaccountably unavailable for service and I find myself with a vacancy for the position." He winked at Malice conspiratorially. "Are you ready to break the Malign oath and start helping other people?"

All eyes fell questioningly on Malice.

"I think," said Malice, looking at her grandad, safely back home with his family, and thinking about all the other grandads they had helped return to their rightful homes that night. "I think it's about time *this* Malign helped look after *other* people's kingdoms, as well as her own."

"That's my girl!" said Grandad.

"Welcome to the private investigating business!" beamed Uncle Vex, holding out his hand for Malice to shake. "I will try my level best to ensure you are not disappeared by ghost-trains, wild-witches, trolls or eagles!"

"How reassuring," chuckled Malice.

"Trolls and witches!" gasped Seth. "Mega cool!"

So Malice began to visit Underland regularly for investigator training with Uncle Vex, which was both interesting and, at times, wonderfully disgusting. Though Ma and Pa didn't entirely approve of her do-gooding, they had to admit she was much better at solving mysteries than she was at making mischief. Since her training began, they had even been known to call upon their daughter's sharp wits when dealing with their more criminally minded haunting recruits.

Seth became Uncle Vex's go-to-guy for super speedy travel around town and assisted their investigating when they were Topside. He continued his moth-whispering lessons with Malice: he could now advise moths that fluttered around hot lightbulbs to fly towards safer lights, such as the moon.

Seth's dads, Bill and Pete Pinkerton, invited Uncle Vex round for tea and they had a smashing time reminiscing about the good old days. Bill was an

inventor and designed some interesting new tools for Uncle Vex to add to his investigator's kit.

With the spell broken, the Cosy Grandad Agency had all their cosy grandads returned and soon had them safely ensconced back in their Topside houses. They were rightly impressed with Uncle Vex's investigative services and paid him a handsome bonus, which he used to buy a new suit and stronger hair gel.

Queenie Florus had so enjoyed having all the grandads over for tea that she sold her Stagnant Stems business to Mrs Dismal and her long luscious hare. And turned her house into:

Queenie Florus's Grandads Club.

There, Queenie, Grandad Florus, the King's Head and nimble Jack entertained grandads all day long with show tunes and charades, and an endless supply of stinging nettle tea and dead-fly biscuits.

Which meant Malice's grandad didn't feel lonely any more when Malice wasn't around. He just popped on down to Queenie Florus's Grandads Club for tea and poker, and was always back in time to hear about Malice's adventures in Underland.

Malice and her ghastly family,
would ~~NOT~~ like to thank:

Jenni *'mischief-maker'* Jennings, Malice's Creator

Hannah *'pesky-pest'* Peck, Malice's Illustrator

Chloe *'scallywag'* Seager, Jenni's Agent

Scholastic *(the ringleaders)*, Jenni's Publisher

Yasmin *'misbehaver'* Morrissey, Jenni's Editor

Andrew *'rabble-rouser'* Biscomb, Jenni's Art Director

Rachel *'rascal'* Lawston, Jenni's Designer

Lauren *'tomfoolery'* Fortune, Jenni's Fiction Publisher

Genevieve *'disobedience-diva'* Herr, Jenni's Copyeditor

Peter *'silly-scamp'* Matthews, Jenni's Editorial Manager

Harriet *'troublemaker'* Dunlea, Jenni's Publicist

Rebecca *'naughty-nuisance'* Gillies, Jenni's Marketer

Clare *'chaos-causer'* Hennessy, Jenni's Production Manager

NAME: Malice Morbid Malign

AGE: 11 ³/₄

PROFESSION: Mischief-Maker
& Amateur Detective.

LIKES: Reading, Bathing, Puzzles.

DISLIKES: Malevolent Mischief, Messy
Bedrooms, Not Helping.

INTERESTING FACT: Malice discovered she
could talk to night creatures when she fell into
one of the sinking-bogs in the Malignant House
grounds, aged 4, and was rescued by two barn
owls and a fox named Darwin, who answered her
cries for help. Once a month she hosts a moonlit
supper-club for the night animals in the old
icehouse near the mausoleum.

NAME: Seth Indiana Pinkerton

AGE: 11 1/4

PROFESSION: Paperboy & Amateur Detective.

LIKES: Skeletons, Cycling, Weirdness.

DISLIKES: Meanness, Ordinary, Bedtime.

INTERESTING FACT: Seth shares the same surname as Allan Pinkerton, the founder of Pinkerton's National Detective Agency in America in 1850 who hired the first ever female detective; Kate Warne.

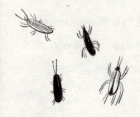

NAME: Antipathy-Rose Malign

AGE: 2

PROFESSION: Mischief-Maker & Biter.

LIKES: Biting, Deep fried pigs' ears, Escaping.

DISLIKES: Dolls with heads, Soft foods,
Grown-ups who talk to her like she's a baby —
even though she is a baby.

INTERESTING FACT: Antipathy-Rose ate her
way through three wicker Moses baskets, four
wooden cribs and a coffin, before Ma finally got
her late lamented pet vultures bird cage down
from the attic for her to sleep in.

NAME: Ma (Tetchy-Sue) Malign

AGE: 32

(actually she is 59, but she's very sensitive about her age. Topunders have a longer life-span than Topsiders because of their magical blood.)

PROFESSION: Mischief-Maker,
CEO of the Malign Haunting Agency.

LIKES: Stink bombs, Earwigs, Swag.

DISLIKES: Cleanliness,
Community spirit, Recycling.

INTERESTING FACT: Ma was taught the delicate art of thievery by the ghost of Diamond Annie, a member of the infamous London all-girl gang called the Forty Elephants, who used to steal jewels and all manner of swag by stuffing it down their big bloomers and underneath their puffy crinoline dresses.

NAME: **Pa (Pugnacious) Malign**

AGE: **66**

PROFESSION: **Mischief-Maker,
Director of the Malign Haunting Agency.**

LIKES: **Stealing, Treasure maps,
Keeping eels in the bath.**

DISLIKES: **Books, Helping, Do-gooders.**

INTERESTING FACT: **In 1987 Pa broke
the world record for the most flies hovering
above a human head. His record was broken
in 1992 by Arthropod Maggot, a Topunder
from the Welsh Borders.**

NAME: **Grandad (Scamp) Rascally**

AGE: **127**

PROFESSION: **Ghost, Merry Mischief-Maker.**

LIKES: **Poker, Stinging nettle tea, Reading.**

DISLIKES: **Malicious mischief, Fuss, Thunderstorms.**

INTERESTING FACT: **In 1908 Grandad worked at the Grand Central Hotel in London and found himself serving breakfast one morning to Emmeline Pankhurst and her fellow suffragettes. He pretended to be polishing teapots so that he could listen to their speeches and has been a feminist ever since.**

NAME: Uncle Vex (Vexatious) Malign

AGE: 58

PROFESSION: Private Underland Investigator.

LIKES: Hair gel, Sharp-suits, Righting wrongs.

DISLIKES: Injustice, Dirty fingernails,
Jack-in-the-boxes.

INTERESTING FACT: Uncle Vex was once
approached by MI5 to join the British intelligence
team. He claims to have turned them down
but Malice has her suspicions that he may
occasionally help them out of a tight spot.

Underland Shopping Guide

NAME: The Vengeful Brew

ESTABLISHED: 1772

TRADE: Tea rooms. Offers — curdled cream teas, curly-edged sandwiches, toxic tea blends.

OWNED BY: Belladonna Nightshade

UNDERLAND LOCATION: Hysteria Lane, The Haunting Quarter.

INTERESTING FACT: Belladonna and her sister Strychnine used to be in a girl band called Hurdy-gurdy & Harp and once played at Hampton Court Palace for Henry VIII.

NAME: The Be-Careful-What-You-Wish-For
Emporium

ESTABLISHED: 1612

TRADE: Purveyor of wishes.

OWNED BY: Blight, Miasma and
Pestilence Shipton.

UNDERLAND LOCATION: 2 Toxicity Mews,
The Haunting Quarter.

INTERESTING FACT: Miasma Shipton was
good chums with Shakespeare and claims that
she and her sisters were his inspiration for the
three witches in his play, *Macbeth*. According to
Miasma, it was she who gave Shakespeare the
line "Double, double toil and trouble."

NAME: The Malign Haunting Agency

ESTABLISHED: 1759 by Irascible Malign

TRADE: Providers of haunting
opportunities and employment

OWNED BY: Ma and Pa Malign

UNDERLAND LOCATION: 2A Toxicity Mews,
The Haunting Quarter.

INTERESTING FACT: The Malign family are
proud to be responsible for many of the hauntings
in Pluckley, said to be the most haunted village in
Britain. With its charming old buildings, Pluckley
is the holiday hotspot for high-flying haunters.

NAME: The Kings Head

ESTABLISHED: 1640

TRADE: Seller of ales, wines and pub-grub.

OWNED BY: Earl Hapless Merriment.

UNDERLAND LOCATION: Guillotine Street,
The Shadow District.

INTERESTING FACT: Earl Hapless earned his
living as a Charles I impersonator. Unfortunately,
he was a bit too good at his job and lost his head in
a case of mistaken identity.

NAME: Lethal Legumes

ESTABLISHED: 1897

TRADE: Vegan coffee shop and light-bites.

OWNED BY: Vlad and Lilith Sharptooth.

UNDERLAND LOCATION: Damnation Lane,
The Shadow District.

INTERESTING FACT:
Vlad and Lilith met at a Vegan Vampire music
festival at Stonehenge in 1975 when they
both had tickets for their favourite rock band
Blackcurrant Not Blood. They ate tofu tacos
under the full moon and at sunrise flew to the
nearby Wookey Hole Caves to sleep.

Shops and Market Stalls

Shops in the Haunting Quarter:

THE VENGEFUL BREW
Tea rooms owned by Belladonna

THE BE-CAREFUL-WHAT-YOU-WISH-FOR-EMPORIUM
Wish store owned by the Shipton witches

THE MALIGN HAUNTING AGENCY
Owned by Ma and Pa.

HEX'S R US
Spell shop

POX & PUS APOTHECARY
Pharmacy

Shops in the Shadow District:

THE KING'S HEAD PUB
Owned by Earl Hapless Merriment

THE DUKE'S HEAD PUB
Owned by the Duke of Gallowsfield

LETHAL LEGUMES
Vegan coffee shop owned by Vlad and Lilith

SNITCH & SNIDE NEWSAGENT'S
BURKE AND HARE B&B.

Shops on Shifty Row
(the Underland equivalent of Saville Row):

FUSTY BALLGOWNS
TOP HAT & WAILS
THE SINISTER SEAMSTRESS
THE HARRIDAN HOTEL

The Underland Market:

STAGNANT STEMS
Queenie's flower stall.

CHARCOAL CHESTNUTS
The burnt chestnut stall.

TAINTED LOAF
The baker's stall.

KRAKEN & CLAWS
The fishmonger's stall.

RANCID ROADKILL
The butcher's stall.

VILE VEG
The vegetable stall.